Philip Gilbert Hamerton

The Mount

Narrative of a Visit to the Site of a Gaulish city on Mount Beuvray

Philip Gilbert Hamerton

The Mount
Narrative of a Visit to the Site of a Gaulish city on Mount Beuvray

ISBN/EAN: 9783337277321

Printed in Europe, USA, Canada, Australia, Japan

Cover: Foto ©Andreas Hilbeck / pixelio.de

More available books at **www.hansebooks.com**

THE MOUNT

AND

AUTUN

THE MOUNT

NARRATIVE OF

A VISIT TO THE SITE OF A GAULISH CITY ON MONT BEUVRAY

WITH A DESCRIPTION OF THE NEIGHBORING
CITY OF

AUTUN

BY

PHILIP GILBERT HAMERTON

AUTHOR OF "THE INTELLECTUAL LIFE," "A PAINTER'S CAMP,"
"ROUND MY HOUSE," "WENDERHOLME," "A SUMMER
VOYAGE ON THE RIVER SAÔNE," ETC.

BOSTON
ROBERTS BROTHERS
1897

University Press:

JOHN WILSON AND SON, CAMBRIDGE, U.S.A.

CONTENTS.

———•———

THE MOUNT.

CHAPTER I.

CHAPTER II.

CHAPTER III.

CHAPTER IV.

CHAPTER V.

CHAPTER VI.

CHAPTER VII.

CHAPTER VIII.

AUTUN.

THE MOUNT.

CHAPTER I.

ON the western side of the valley or basin
of Autun, rises a massive hill, about
1,800 feet above the level of the plain, and
2,700 above the sea-level. It plays a great
part in all effects of sunset, being remote
enough to take fine blue or purple color in
certain conditions of the atmosphere. The
distance from my house is about ten miles as
the crow flies, or it is twenty miles by road,
so that the hill may be reached in a drive, and

I go there from time to time, yet not so frequently as a certain friend of mine, who has reasons of his own 'for taking an especial interest in Mount Beuvray.

The best way to initiate the reader into the peculiar charms and characteristics of the Mount, is to take him with me, if he will kindly pardon the liberty, and let the place come upon him gradually, as it would upon an actual traveller. He shall, however, in addition, possess certain advantages which are only shared by very few and highly-favored pilgrims of the Mount.

Before we start, I will just whet the reader's appetite with the remark, which he will find fully justified before we have done, that Mount Beuvray is, much more than any other hill or mountain that I have either visited or read about, a place of peculiar characteristics. It has not the grandeur of my old friend, Ben Cruachan, and, as for height, its whole elevation is but the *difference* between Mont Blanc and the Aiguille Verte; yet the impression that Ben Cruachan leaves is essentially what you will receive after climbing several other Highland mountains, and the exploration of glaciers on Mont Blanc has just the same

kind of interest as the exploration of glaciers
in other regions of the Alps. But every one
who knows the Beuvray remembers it as we
remember some very original being, for there
are not two Beuvrays, either in France or
elsewhere.

There lives at Autun a friend of mine, who
shall be called in these pages the Antiquary;
and sometimes we arrange to go to the
Beuvray together. Let me take one of these
excursions as an example of the rest.

It has sometimes been said that the French
are an inhospitable nation, but if this is a rule
it is a rule with a good many very striking
exceptions, and the Antiquary is one of them.
It is settled that I am to go and fetch him for
a drive to the Beuvray, and take my four-
wheeled dog-cart, because he has some *impedi-
menta* of awkward shape and size which he is
anxious to transport to the Mount. These
turn out to be a deal table about seven feet
long, with trestles, and a few little personal effects. As for me, I too have things to carry —
namely, a knapsack and general artistic equip-
ment for the purpose of studying from nature.
We intend to stay nearly a week on the
Mount, so I burden myself in addition with a

small sack of corn and several trusses of hay.
The deal table with the trestles, the trusses of
hay, and my saddle are arranged and corded
behind the dog-cart, giving it anything but an
elegant appearance ; indeed it may be doubted
whether an English gentleman would have
courage to drive through an English town on
a vehicle loaded in that manner, but as we
two are people who have our own purposes in
view, and regard public opinion with the most
contemptuous indifference, we do not trouble
our minds with reflections about what the
French Mrs. Grundy may say. The Antiquary's town residence, where I go to fetch
him, is one of the best in the little city. You
enter the garden under the shadow of a great
porte-cochère with oak doors large enough to
admit a wain of hay, and the porter's lodge in
the sides of the structure and above it. Once
inside, you find yourself in a garden over-
shadowed by magnificent trees, most notably
by one gigantic acacia, certainly the finest I
ever beheld. My little mare, whose name is
Cocotte, is unharnessed and led to the stable
through a building which is quite a museum,
being full of massive remnants of antiquity,
such as capitals of columns, big stones with

inscriptions, old fireplaces, and niches, and other objects of embarrassing dimensions that antiquaries love to collect, and don't know where to put when they have collected them. Cocotte passes through the museum alike without damaging anything or observing anything, and arrives at last at a certain stall in the stable, already perfectly well known to her. The coach-house, too, is crammed with antiquities, for the Antiquary does not keep a carriage, partly because it would turn out his big stones, the ugliest of which is lovelier in his eyes than the most elegant of Parisian vehicles.

The Antiquary has a large state dining-room adorned with old carved oak and a choice collection of old French and Italian ware, but he has also a smaller dining-room, for ordinary occasions, furnished in the simple way that the French people like for a " room to eat in." Here we have a little *déjeuner* as a preparation for the labors of the day. It is now ten o'clock ; we have been both hard at work since six, and are ready to do honor to our repast.

A Frenchman always seems gayer and brighter at *déjeuner* than at dinner-time, and he is never so hospitable as at a *déjeuner* without ceremony. Ours passes as pleasantly as can be; we talk of the journey before us, settle the detail of our little arrangements, and perhaps enjoy the good cookery and perfect service all the better from the knowledge that we have a rougher existence before us, and are bidding a temporary farewell to these refinements of an elaborate civilization.

My host is one of those few and enviable people who have managed, in their own peculiar way, to lead the ideal life. It may not be exactly your ideal, reader; it is not exactly mine; for it is the peculiarity of every truly ideal life that it is strongly individual, and not fashioned on a model that would precisely fit anybody else. My host lives in the past; in him the historical and antiquarian sense predominates over the feeling that goes with the current of the world's diurnal existence. I have often seen him read old books, but never a newspaper, and once I asked him whether he ever *did* read such a thing as a newspaper, when he answered " No," with the greatest decision. History is his delight, politics his abhorrence. He does not see that the newspaper, amongst its tiresome discussions of

small matters that will be forgotten in a few
weeks or months, does really at the same time
contain the history of the current year, so that
if the historical sense embraced the present as
well as the past, it would read *The Times* as well
as Tacitus. Forgetting one day that my friend
never opened a newspaper, I happened to
make an allusion to the siege of Carthagena,
when he told me that he was not aware that
Carthagena had been besieged at all, or specially occupied by the Spanish communards,
and he did not seem grateful for the information, but, if anything, slightly put out by having to hear what had been read by another
person in a newspaper. Some contemporary
events do, however, reach him by their very
loudness. If a powder-magazine exploded in
the next street, he would probably become
aware of the circumstance in the privacy of
his own study, and in the same manner he got
to know that there was a war between France
and Prussia, and that the capital of France
was surrounded by a German army. Since
the departure of the Germans he has heard
from some friends of his that Thiers has been
succeeded by Marshal MacMahon, and, to my
great surprise, he evidently was aware that

the Duc de Broglie was at one time Prime
Minister. He knew something of the attempt
to restore Henri V., but that was because a
near relation of his was a friend of the exiled
Prince, and in correspondence with Frohsdorf,
whither he went on a pilgrimage, to be close
to the person of his sovereign. It is needless
to add that the contemporary history of neighboring countries is a blank in my friend's
mind, but he knows nearly all that is to be
known about their condition from the time
of Cæsar to the end of the fifteenth century.
Yet although my friend's knowledge of antiquity is bought at the cost of this ignorance
of the present, it is well worth the sacrifice,
for thousands of people know the contents of
the newspapers, for one who keeps alive the
record of bygone generations. If I want to
learn the names of the men who composed
the last French Ministry, the idlers in the
nearest café can tell me ; but if I want accurate
knowledge about some epoch in the past history of the very locality where these idlers
live, they cannot tell me. The human race
may, therefore, well afford that a few scattered
antiquaries here and there should be careless
of the present that they may be careful of the

too easily and readily forgotten past. It is
they who, by labors of infinite patience, rewarded always by the ridicule of their neigh-
bors, preserve the chain of the world's history
and have even been so successful as to restore
many a missing link.

Not only is the Antiquary sufficiently independent of public opinion to remain content-
edly ignorant of newspapers, but in his ways
of life, as the reader will abundantly learn
before he comes to the close of this narrative,
my antiquarian friend has had the courage
and wisdom to follow his own taste and gov-
ern his expenditure on principles in harmony
with his own character and pursuits. Thus,
in his house, there are what may be called a
set of state apartments, furnished as an artist
with antiquarian tastes, or an antiquary with
artistic tastes, might be expected to furnish
them. There is a certain tendency towards
magnificence here and there, but never of the
vulgar kind, and every object has its character
and history. No upholsterer had the furnishing of these rooms, but the owner gradually
gathered round him things at the same time
rich and beautiful and possessing some historical interest. His drawing-rooms are, in fact, a

museum that you may live in, or a habitation
that you may study in. The mirrors are old
Venetian glass with the rich Italian frame; the
time-piece is a curious example, and very
elegant, of the earliest French workmanship
of that kind; the busts are antique marbles;
the books on the table are illuminated manuscripts of the middle ages. But the real
museum, for of course the Antiquary has a
museum, consists of a large room and a gallery upstairs, full of accumulated treasures
from antiquity down to the sixteenth century,
but especially and peculiarly rich in remnants
of Gaulish workmanship and the workmanship of the Roman occupants of Gaul. The
whole of this has been gathered by and for
the historical and artistic sense, never for vulgar luxury, and, although the Antiquary has
plenty of roomy armchairs covered with tapestry or velvet, I have seen him, for a week
together, use nothing but a hard wooden stool
without either a cushion or a back to it. So
with cookery; as the Antiquary is a giver of
good dinners, he cannot in his town house do
without the services of an accomplished cook,
but anywhere else he is perfectly contented
with a basin of soup or a piece of bread and

an egg, and can alter all his habits as easily
as a soldier accustomed to the changes and
chances of war-time. This is a very uncom-
mon faculty in a man of his age, for he is
nearly sixty, especially when men so well
advanced in life have every luxury at their
command that self-indulgence pets itself with.

After *déjeuner* we set off on our expedition,
driving on a good road under a burning sun,
with a fair landscape on every side in the
freshness of the beginning of June. For me
there is always plenty of entertainment in
driving through a picturesque country even
without a companion, but the pleasure is
much enhanced when one has a companion
able to appreciate everything on the way,
and well acquainted with the history of the
localities.

The first village we came to, called Monthelon, is very celebrated in French ecclesiastical
history as having been for some years the
residence of an excellent lady whose reputation
for goodness was so great that it survived her,
and more than a hundred years after her death
was still so powerful that Pope Clement XIII.
canonized her as a saint. She was married to
Christophe de Rabutin, Baron of Chantal, in

1592, and eight years afterwards her husband
was accidentally killed by a friend of his when
out hunting. He left her with six children,
and she came to the château at Monthelon,
where she stayed seven years and a half with
her husband's father. Her early widowhood
seems to have led to a remarkable religious
development in her mind, and the rest of her
life was passed in educating her family and
attending to the poor. Saint François de Sales
came to Monthelon and told her of his project
for the establishment of an order to be called
the Order of the Visitation. She entered
heartily into this scheme, and in 1610 left
Monthelon to go to Annecy, that she might
help in carrying it out practically. From all
that I have been able to learn of her, she was
one of those good women whom everybody
must respect, notwithstanding religious differences. Her memory is kept perfectly alive by
her own church, and there are occasionally
pilgrimages to Monthelon, though it is not so
fashionable as Lourdes or Paray-le-Monial,
because she was not so miraculous a personage as Marie Alacoque, nor is Monthelon a
place of miracles like Lourdes. It is a very
interesting little place, however, and the

château the good Baronne de Chantal lived
in is still in general aspect quite what it was
in her time. There is a chapel at the north
end which in the interior is nothing but a
narrow room, very high proportionately to its
breadth, but the chapel has a belfry and buttresses outside, as well as a porch, which give
it an ecclesiastical aspect. These have been
lately restored, — in other words, the old belfry
was pulled down and a new one built in its
place, but this last is a faithful copy of the
original. The spire is one of those that spread
out suddenly at the bottom like the rim of a
peaked hat. Another interesting architectural
feature is an open gallery in the house itself
which is simply a corridor left free to the air
by an opening in the wall extending its whole
length, the roof being here supported by short
columns. It is surprising how very valuable
is this simple device from the architectural
point of view, as the columns catch the light
and a broad shadow always lurks somewhere
in the corridor itself. The staircase is exterior
also up to the first floor, arrangements bor-
rowed from southern custom, and convenient
in the latitude only during a third of the year.
It is pleasant in the summer evening or early

morning to get a little fresh air as you pass
from one room to another in the open, but not
quite so agreeable when the cold blasts gather
furiously in the corridor in the depth of a
Morvan winter   Seen from the opposite side,
the château presents the usual appearance of
houses of that class with massive round towers
at the angles and large picturesque dormer
windows in the roof; but notwithstanding its
apparent size it is a most inconvenient place
to live in.   Some one suggested to me a few
years ago that I might get it on lease; and
the situation was very attractive, for it is in a
lovely valley near a pure and beautiful stream,
but although the house was not in very bad
repair, and there were several large habitable
rooms, the arrangement of them was so excessively inconvenient that we abandoned the
idea after one visit.   The place belongs to
the Prince de Montholon, who takes an interest in its preservation, and it is inhabited at
present by a farmer and dealer in bark for
tanning, who leaves everything just as he
found it.   The tenant most to be dreaded for
a place like this is a rich *bourgeois* with a passion for neat windows, tidy slate roofs, and
iron railings.

There is a remarkable little church at Monthelon of the pure Romanesque type, which always seems to me the most suitable kind of architecture for a village church when there is not much money to be laid out. Unfortunately these little old Romanesque churches are rapidly disappearing all over the country, for whenever they are out of repair, and nothing is easier than to let an old structure fall into that state, the *curé* is seized with an ardent ambition to get rid of his old church altogether and build a gaunt new edifice in place of it, of the most meagre Gothic that poverty in money and poverty in ideas can together realize. What I like so much in the little old Romanesque buildings is their total absence of false pretension, their substantial strength, and their perfect snugness. The transition from the substantial old cottages, centuries old, to the little Romanesque church is so natural that the peasant must feel as much at home in one as in the other, whereas a church that seems as if it had been picked up in some new American town and set down again in the middle of a quaint old Morvan village is a glaring incongruity — for the present. The only consolation is that in twenty years the villages will be as new and ugly as the churches. To my taste, however, there is nothing in village architecture to be compared with the chancel and apse of such a building as that at Monthelon, so simple and yet so complete, so substantial in rustic strength, and yet at the same time so full of satisfactions for the artistic sense in pleasant changes of curves in their perspective, and various light and shade. Even the priest himself, if he could but think so, looks far more effective when officiating in a tiny chancel that is like an oratory, than he ever can do under a lofty roof, make himself as gorgeous as he may. In the great cathedrals the effort of the Roman clergy to struggle against the overwhelming immensity of their architectural surroundings is never more than half successful; the height of a man is not sufficient for the purpose, though he blaze with gold and jewels. The mitre and crosier add something, the banner and cross still more, yet when all is done the priests look like mice on the floor of a room.

There was an old priest at Monthelon who lived in great simplicity, but sometimes re-

ceived visits from curés in the neighborhood.
Two of these came to see him on one occasion and stayed to a frugal *déjeuner*. After
they were gone, the old man fell asleep with
his feet close to the blazing logs upon the
hearth, and his wooden shoes unfortunately
took fire; but the curé went on sleeping still,
and he did not awake until his feet were
rather badly burnt. The incident in itself
is at the same time very ludicrous and very
painful, — the idea of the curé reclining tran-
quilly in his easy-chair whilst his wooden
shoes were burning with the logs, is just one
of those ideas that Goya would have delighted
to illustrate in his fearful caricatures; but
the matter did not end there. The popular
rumor, always rather malicious about ecclesiastics, took up the matter in its own way,
and set it abroad that the two curés who had
been there to *déjeuner* had rewarded their
entertainer by forcibly putting his feet into
the fire in the fun of a drunken frolic. One
of the two felt so hurt by the currency of these
stories that he took the trouble to contradict
them in the pulpit, but with a result entirely
different from what he intended; for, as he
told me himself, the peasants who heard him

went about saying that he had made a full
confession.   It is wonderful how difficult it is
to correct a popular impression even in classes
very superior to the French peasantry.[1]   The
old curé whose feet were burnt had some curious oddities or originalities.   He was fond of
putting Latin into his sermons, a little bit at
a time, his own Latin, not of the best.   Here
is an authentic extract in the original tongues,
for of course it would be entirely spoilt by
any attempt at translation.

"Lorsque je paraîtrai devant Notre Seigneur il
me demandera 'Curé Monthelon ius ubi sunt bre-
betis meis' — ce qui veut dire 'Curé de Monthelon
où sont mes brebis,' et moi je lui répondrai 'Bêtes
je les ai trouvées, bêtes je les ai laissées, et bêtes
elles sont probablement encore.'"

The good priest was not more complimen-
tary in his French than classical in his Latin.

---

[1] I remember a curious instance of this in England.   There
was an impression, amongst the upper classes, that insanity
had been prevalent in a certain family, and this was asserted
to be the case on the authority of a certain historian whose
name was used as evidence; yet that historian had never
printed any assertion to that effect.   In the same way, nothing
is more common than for things to be believed to be in the
Bible which are not in the Bible, though almost every Englishman has a copy of it.

After leaving this little village we came to
a pond that had been intentionally dried up,
and my companion told me the reason, which is
worth mentioning. Somebody had planted in
it an aquatic plant called *cornuelle* in French;
the botanical name of it is *Trapa natans*,
and it belongs to the family of *Halorageæ*.
I am not aware that it has an English name.
This plant produces an edible fruit, a sort of
nut, from which comes another of its popular
names, the *châtaigne d'eau*, and the country
people make use of it at home or carry it to
market as a salable article of consumption.
The fruit is farinaceous and sweet; it may be
made into a sort of porridge, and bread appears to have been made from it in ancient
times. The only objection to the plant is
that, when once it has taken root in a pond,
it soon gets possession of the whole water,
which is entirely invaded and occupied by it.
Nothing can be done with the pond afterwards except to drain it and cultivate the
ground as a field, for even if after the lapse
of years the place is put under water again
the *cornuelle* reappears almost immediately,
as some root fibres are sure to remain in the
earth. The dry pond we passed had been

permanently abandoned as a hopeless enter-
prise, which says a good deal for the power of
one aquatic weed in its contest against the
energy of man ; for a fish-pond is a very productive property in this country, — more productive than dry land when the land is not
of the best quality and the pond can be made
without too large an expenditure of capital
on an expensive dam.

The castle or tower of Vautheau, which we
came upon rather later, is one of the most perfect examples of the feudal castle in Burgundy,
and the remaining tower is in that happy
condition between repair and ruin when nothing has been spoiled for the eye, either by
time or meddlesome repairs. The roof is still
there, the door is still locked, but nobody lives
in the rooms. The rest of the castle is a ruin.
My companion the Antiquary proposed one
of his brilliant ideas which he is quite the man
to carry into execution. He proposed to rent
the tower from its owner merely for the pleasure of furnishing one room perfectly with the
old mediæval things from his own collection,
and if he does this, which I have good hopes
he will, that room will produce quite perfectly
the illusion of a return to the real middle

ages, so far as the picturesque is concerned.
He enumerated to me all the treasures that he
could spare for its adornment, certainly making in the aggregate a much richer plenishing
than the room ever knew in the times of its
mighty seigneurs; for my friend proposed to
himself, as people generally do in such projects, rather the realization of an ideal than
the literal restoration of a bygone reality.
There are two good chambers in the tower
that might be treated in this manner, and if
ever the scheme is carried out, the Antiquary
will possess a rare half-way house between his
town residence and the Mount, dividing the
distance just equally, and thus affording him
an excellent excuse for sleeping in the midst
of his treasures. It is an antiquary's fancy,
but it might equally be a poet's fancy, or a
painter's. The tower itself is a perfect un-
spoiled gem, rich with its own beauty and the
beauty of the most magnificent ivy I ever
beheld, whilst the cluster of old cottages near
the castle, the elegant Renaissance pigeon
tower with its dome and crown of columns,
the magnificent chestnuts that abound in the
neighborhood and the glorious breadths of
landscape to be seen from there, would occupy

a painter for many a summer's day.   The poet
or story-teller would find suggestions in the
ancient history and legends of the place.
Jacques, Sire de Vautheau, was a zealous
Huguenot in times when it needed the heroic
temper to profess any shade of Protestantism
here, and he held preachings within the walls
of his castle which were attended by "seven
hundred gentlemen and damsels."   It is said
too, by historians of the opposite party, that in
his zeal for his own faith he rode out frequently
from Vautheau with a band of Calvinist sol-
diers and pillaged the churches round about.
Jean de Traves, of this family, made prisoner
a bishop of Châlons in 1545 who was also the
confessor of Cardinal de Medicis, on his way
to the Council of Trent.   But in 1653 the
zeal of Protestantism must have come to an
end in this family, for the Count of Vautheau
was present at the solemn entry of a new
bishop into Autun.   Very near the castle, in a
beautiful hollow, under the shade of magnificent old trees lies a well bordered by wild-
flowers, and, being thirsty, I went to this cool
spring to drink.   On this the Antiquary said,
" Mind you take the diamond if the opportunity presents itself, but you must be quick

and careful, or else your fate will be terrible."
I thought, "Here is some old legend, but
I can wait to hear it till I have slaked my
thirst"; so, having drunk heartily of the pure
cool water, I rejoined my friend and he resumed the subject of the diamond.

"One of the most ancient legends in France
is connected with that well where you have
just been drinking, and the peasants all believe in it firmly to this day. It is the fountain of the Wivre,[1] which is a supernatural
serpent that always carries about with him a
diamond of prodigious value. He comes to
this well to drink, and whenever he does so
he is obliged to lay down his diamond. Now
if anybody happens to be there when the serpent comes, and is quick enough to seize the
diamond just when the serpent is drinking,
and get away with it before the serpent has
slaked his thirst, then he will become the richest man in the whole world; but if the Wivre
perceives that he is robbed, he will instantly
slay the unsuccessful thief. However, as you

---

[1] Pronounced *Vivre*, of course, in French. I wonder if
there is any connection between this word and the name of
the heraldic monster Wivern. It appears highly probable
that there must be some connection, as the words are so very
nearly identical.

have come back alive, and do not look as if
you had just got possession of a great diamond,
I infer that the Wivre did not happen to visit
his well at the same time with you."

The legend of the Wivre is very persistent
in these regions, and reappears in other forms.
It is the old story of the dragon or serpent
guardian, whose treasures may not be got at
without the utmost peril. We shall find the
Wivre again elsewhere, at a distance from his
well.

CHAPTER II.

WE stayed half an hour at St. Léger-sous-Beuvray, an old village in the midst of beautiful scenery. There are two old manor-houses in this village, with towers, and in the bottom of the valley lies a beautiful little lake sheltered by hills of some boldness and elevation, with a fine view of Mount Beuvray that reflects itself in the water just as mountains do in the true lake districts. Indeed, by the help of a little imagination it is not difficult in this place to imagine oneself in some part of Southern Scotland or Wales. A ramble from this lake to the village of St. Léger, along a rough bridle path that passes through a farmyard, is one of the most picturesque little walks I remember anywhere. The buildings seem to have been erected on purpose to be painted, and there are groves of gigantic chestnuts. Indeed, the neighborhood of the Beuvray — and the rising grounds here are nothing but the advanced buttresses of the Mount — is remarkable for the number and size of its ancient chestnuts, of all trees the most nobly pictorial; but my companion the Antiquary, who has always something disagreeable to tell me about the tasteless destructiveness of his contemporaries, says that within his own recollection great numbers of the finest old trees have disappeared, and he can point to many a situation now sadly denuded where formerly stood families of giant brethren, casting large breadths of shade. However, there is still many a corner about the Beuvray that neither the axe of the woodman nor the hideous erection of the modern mason has ruined by destruction or addition, — places where poet might ramble, or painter sketch, without shutting his eyes to anything.

The village of St. Léger is remarkable for
one of the most terrible incidents in the history of animal life. Wolves, like dogs, are
subject to hydrophobia, and on the 18th of
June, 1718, at nightfall, the place was visited
by a mad wolf from the top of the Beuvray that
wounded and disfigured no less than sixteen
people, of whom all but one died of hydrophobia. The single exception was a woman who
had only been scratched by the animal's claws.
After this incident a confraternity of St. Hu-
bert was established, in connection with the
church and by the authority of the bishop, for
the destruction of wild beasts. This is a curious example of a hunt established by episcopal authority, and in the closest connection
with religion. Another mad wolf came down
from the Beuvray on the eve of Pentecost,
some time in the last century, and, having
already bitten a shepherdess and several cows
on the hill, attacked three men in a hamlet on
the other side, grievously injuring one of
them. This is a thing the wolf never does,
when in his ordinary health and senses.

Between the village of St. Léger and the
Mount, the road passes through scenery of
almost unimaginable richness. Beautiful

slopes are wooded with noble trees, and there
is an elegance in the lines of the hills in the
highest degree delightful to the artistic sense.
There is wood enough, and of the most majes-
tic kind, but there is not too much wood;
you see beautiful meadows with fine shadows
lengthening down their slopes, and plenty of
open spaces for the golden sunshine to dwell
upon.   This is one of those very rare localities where there is absolutely nothing to
offend the most fastidious taste, — scenery as
rich as it can be in beautiful forms of earth
and magnificent vegetation of ancient trees,
without anything whatever to spoil it.   Under
the warm-toned afternoon sunshine it looked
like some poet's dream of Arcady, the beautiful hills, one behind another, leading the eye
on and on till it rested upon the dim blue
land beyond the Loire.

   To the right of this rose the Mount, a great
shapely mass, not a mountain with rocky sum-
mits and ravines scooped out by the floods of
innumerable years, but a beautifully formed hill
clothed to the very top with forest; at least
so it appeared from the vale in which we were
travelling, but happily there are still spaces
clear of trees.   I say "happily," because noth-

ing so completely destroys all enjoyment of a hill or mountain as a dense wood all over it. There is another hill in this country, higher than the Beuvray, from which the views would be magnificent if any one might be permitted to behold them; but the trees make this an impossibility, and you might as well bury yourself in some lowland plantation as climb that lofty height.

The high-road goes over a sort of *col*, as a Swiss would call it, rising steadily till it comes to the pass and then descending on the other side for several miles. In this way, at least half the ascent is made before we know that we have begun it. Few of the excellent high-roads that were made all over France forty years ago have produced a more beneficial change than these good roads in the hilly district of the Morvan. Before they were executed, many parts of the district were only accessible on horseback or in the rude bullock-cart of the peasantry, and the consequence of such difficult communication was brigandage. The neighborhood of the Beuvray was especially inaccessible, from the abrupt character of the minor hills which form its buttresses, and from the wild situations of the hamlets that are scattered round it. One has the impression, a quite involuntary impression, that a road has existed forever; it seems, like a river, to be one of the natural arteries of the world, and when we find buildings by the roadside, we conclude at once that they were erected there for the convenience that the road afforded, when the truth very often is that the buildings are of much earlier date, and the road has come there since, greatly to their advantage, yet without intentional consideration of it. An excellent illustration of this is a cluster of most picturesque farm buildings where we stayed to leave the carriage just before reaching the *col.* They were probably four hundred years old, perhaps older, and for at least three centuries and a half out of that time they must have remained an isolated tenement on the slope of a wild Morvan hill, accessible only by some rocky or tortuous bridle-path. The nineteenth century brings a broad highway to the very door, and so the buildings immediately begin to look as if they had been erected for convenience of access to it, losing half their character in consequence. How subtly dependent is the effect of everything upon its surroundings!

In a narrative of travel I think it is always

worth while to set down, not only what happens to you, but what you learn; for surely
the latter is the chief result, since it remains
with you permanently afterwards. The Antiquary and I had a conversation about architecture and the work of modern architects,
whilst the things were being transferred from
the carriage to a rude cart that was to take
them up the hill. Our talk was suggested
by a range of buildings that seemed to me
well worth drawing. Why was it worth
drawing? How was it that rude unlettered
peasants, centuries ago, could design an interesting building when the clever educated
architects in modern towns only design
things that make an artist shut his eyes, or
look in another direction? Well, to begin
with, the old building was full of the most
beautiful and delicate curvature. The sky
line was in curves, the lines of the eaves were
in curves, graceful as the hanging of a gar-
land, and the curious felicity of these forms
was unexpected, being suggested only by
convenience wherever they occurred. There
was a window high in the wall, so the eaves
took a leap over it, graceful as the flight of
a swallow when it passes over a hedge. One

end of the building rested against the hill-
side, so the eaves hung down from it like
a chain, and there was just one piece of quite
regular mathematical curvature as a climax,
— the arch of a doorway in good stone, with
mouldings.   Then there was plenty of light
and shade, — shadows cast from projecting
roofs or nestling in cool recesses, lights
catching brilliantly on pieces of woodwork
or gray stone, and losing themselves along
the rough surface of the walls.   The color,
too, was perfectly harmonious, all in beautiful grays, with dark purples and browns,
nothing discordant or offensive anywhere.
"Now suppose," said my friend the Antiquary, "a misfortune which in these days
is only too likely to happen. Suppose that
the owner of this beautiful old building were
to take it into his head that he would like
a new one better, and so pull it all down
and erect what he would consider a handsome new building in its place. You would
have a roof in glaring red tiles without one
curve in it anywhere, a flat rectangular wall
without a shadow, and every line either vertical
or horizontal except the perspective of the tiles,
which would be like a perspective diagram in
a handbook of elementary science."

I had taken the precaution to put a saddle
in the carriage, so Cocotte was soon trans-
formed into a saddle-horse, and in this guise
began the last ascent. We were soon buried
in the woods on a narrow road that climbed at
first in zigzags and afterwards in a straighter
line. The road was just broad enough for
the wheels of the cart that carried our baggage; but the Antiquary took a much deeper
interest in it than in the fine high-road that
we had left, for this was a Gaulish road
that had existed before the Roman invasion.
There are several such roads on Mount Beuvray, all of them leading to the summit.
After a good deal of climbing we emerged
from the wood and found ourselves upon
an elevated shoulder of the hill, between a
deep dell to the left and a great projecting
spur of the mountain to the right with a
rock pinnacle at the point of it, and now we
had views over a great stretch of country.
" That rock," said the Antiquary, " is the rock
of the Wivre, at whose well you drank as we
came along. I will tell you more about it
afterwards."

The narrow road plunged again into the
wood, and soon became very steep indeed.

I am a little in advance of the Antiquary
and the cart, for he has requested me to
ride forward and order dinner.

Order dinner on the top of Mount Beuvray? Yes, very decidedly; and I know
perfectly well where to order it, for this is
not the first time that I have climbed up
into this elevated region. I keep on up the
steep road till within a hundred yards of
the summit, and then turn aside to the
right, along another narrow way amongst
the trees, and suddenly come upon the Antiquary's own mountain establishment, the
loftiest habitation in Burgundy.

A few words of description are necessary
in this place, for without them the reader
would never guess what sort of a mansion
was prepared for our reception. First, there
is a large clear space enclosed by wooden
railings and sheltered from the wind by the
summit of the hill, which rises steeply to
the east, for we are not *quite* on the top
yet, though very near it.

At one end of this cleared ground stand
two wooden huts, and a stone cottage between them with a thatched roof. At the
other end there is a thatched shed with two

divisions. This is my friend's encampment.
The stone cottage is a recent development
of luxury, built a year or two since, but I
knew the encampment in its first begin-
nings. It began with a single wooden hut,
the smaller of the two that still exist. Next,
a rude little wigwam was erected for a domestic, but the rain got into the wigwam, and
it was thought inhuman to make him sleep
there; so a second hut was built, larger and
more commodious. This accounts for the
two huts, and the establishment was limited
to them for some seasons, except when I
added a tent of my own to it; but there
is a law which governs all permanent camps
which the Antiquary could no more escape
than anybody else. A camp is kept in the
true camp condition only by being moved from
place to place. Once fixed, it soon becomes a
camp no longer. You begin, let us say, with
a tent, — a genuine tent, that can be struck
or erected in a few minutes. If you are on
the move, your tent will remain a tent, and its
portable quality will be appreciated; but if
you fix your camp in one spot, you will soon
have a wooden floor to your tent, next you
will elevate it on wooden walls, and finally

you will have a hut. There is a vast difference in comfort between a tent and a hut, so
that if you are fixed the hut becomes inevitable. For a year or two you will remain satisfied with your wooden walls, but there are
certain objections to the best of huts, especially when they get rather old, and the next
thing you dream of will be a stone cottage.
The climax of your improvements will be
a mansion, if you are rich enough to build
one on the spot, and I have actually seen
this done in the Highlands; I have seen the
rough cottage, where the sportsmen enjoyed
themselves infinitely, replaced by a lordly
shooting-lodge, where they enjoyed themselves less because the good house brought
with it all the exigencies of etiquette. The
Antiquary has reached the cottage state now,
but it is a genuine rough cottage, and not
what is called a cottage at Scarborough or
Brighton.

I stop at the entrance to the rude enclosure
and call out vigorously, " Pauchard." The
door of the cottage opens, and Pauchard
makes his appearance with an exclamation
of delight, throwing up both hands into the
air, and running towards me with many

words of welcome. Pauchard is cook, house-keeper, butler, chambermaid, etc., to the Antiquary when he lives on the Mount, and in all these functions eminent for a combination of zeal, rapidity, and discretion beyond praise. He is a little man, a very little man, but built like a little Hercules, and as active as he is strong. A more cheerful, good-tempered, affectionate, and perfectly reliable servant was master never blessed with.

Pauchard and I are great friends, but I know my place too well to imagine that his exclamation of delight was entirely for myself. One third of it was for me, two thirds for Cocotte. He likes me, he loves Cocotte, and she returns this affection with all the tenderness the equine nature is capable of; certainly she prefers Pauchard to her master.

Cocotte is soon at liberty to wander about the hill at her pleasure, — we know that she will not wander far. Pauchard sets to work heartily with his pans in the kitchen; the cart arrives with our luggage and the deal table, and we busy ourselves in getting things in order.

The cottage is a substantial little building, entirely in granite, and containing a couple

of rooms, one of them rather capacious, for
the master, the other smaller, for Pauchard
and his pans. The Antiquary, whose town
mansion is finished with pretty inlaid *parquets*
that nobody but a barbarian would walk upon
in anything but dress boots, has judged, with
perfect taste and good sense, that his mountain cell must be organized on quite different
principles. There is no French polish here.
The joists in the ceiling are all visible, and of
oak simply planed, over them a boarding of
oak also, just planed but no more. The
granite walls are covered with one coating
of rough mortar, but no finish of plaster.
The chimney-piece consists of three huge
blocks of stone, almost as rude as the constructions at Stonehenge. The only luxury
is a wooden floor, but we may walk upon it
with nailed boots if we like. The tables are
deal boards supported on trestles. Some
shelves and two cupboards complete the furnishing. Stay — I had forgot the chairs —
stools with hard wooden seats and no backs.
The Antiquary sits on one of these, without
desiring more luxurious rest; but after a hard
day's walking upon the Mount, I borrow a
rush-bottomed chair of Pauchard, for he has

two of them in his kitchen, and, like other rich men, can only use one of his luxuries at once.

My first request is for a glass of water, such water as no Londoner or Parisian ever drinks. Close to the cottage there is a fountain, a pure perennial spring, filling a clean little reservoir of about a cubic yard, cut in the living rock, and arched over with antique masonry. The water is as clear as the air, and always cold, even in this hot weather. To my taste, the perfect purity and inexhaustible abundance of this and other fountains on the Beuvray are among its chief delights. There is no such water anywhere in the plains, and, do what you will by filtering and icing, you can never imitate the cold clear fountains that flow from that mother of all purity, the granite.

The Antiquary, being a Burgundian, does not half appreciate his fountain as he ought. He talks of it, indeed, with the grace of Virgil and the enthusiasm of Theocritus, but the fountain from which he drinks is of another nature. There is a little cavern, well guarded by a strong door with great iron bars and locks, and in this cavern sleeps many a bottle

of the choicest Burgundian vintages.   I drink
more water in a day than the Antiquary does
in six months, but I do it in secret whenever
possible, for when my host catches me in the
act a grave reproof is sure to follow.   He is
quite seriously persuaded that water is most
dangerous, and that the vine is the only
spring from which man may drink in safety.

CHAPTER III.

A REASON FOR THE ANTIQUARY'S SOJOURNS ON THE MOUNT
— ANCIENT FORTIFICATIONS — THE MOUNT FORMERLY
THE SITE OF A STRONG HILL CITY — ANTIQUARIAN DIG-
GINGS — OUR MANNER OF LIVING ON THE MOUNT —
THE CHIMNEY — INSCRIPTIONS — TAPESTRY — A SERE-
NADE TO THE ANTIQUARY — THE AUTHOR'S FIRST VISIT
TO THE MOUNT.

AND now, whilst Pauchard is cooking our dinner, let me take this opportunity of explaining why we are here at all, — why the huts and the cottages are here. It is not simply for the pleasure of seeing an extensive prospect that the Antiquary climbs the Mount once a week throughout the summer, and every summer, year after year. The beautiful Mount is a delightful place to visit, but an occasional excursion would suffice to keep its beauties in the memory. Evidently there must be another reason for the Antiquary's singular persistence.

Yes, there *is* a reason. Far below the cottage, a great rampart encircles the hill

like a belt; a rampart not merely traceable
by the eye of a keen-sighted Antiquary, but
in many parts as visible, and as large, as a
modern railway embankment. This rampart
is about four miles in circuit, and the whole
of the space within it was occupied, before
the Roman invasion of Gaul, by a strong hill
city. Now the work that my friend has been
pursuing here for the last eight years is the
investigation of this city by means of the
pickaxe and the spade. He has a little body
of laborers under him, who go on steadily
from spring to autumn, and when he encamped here at first it was for the convenience of superintending them and directing
the work better than he could by occasional
visits. The work has been very fruitful, and
is pursued in the most systematic manner.
At every new start a deep trench is dug from
the rampart towards the centre of the city,
and whenever the workmen come upon a
building they go round it and isolate it completely. More than two hundred buildings,
for the most part Gaulish houses, have been
discovered and cleared in this manner, and
whilst the men were doing this they found a
great quantity of portable objects, such as

coins, pottery, jewelry, etc., which are now
lodged in the Museum of St. Germain, for
the most part, though a selection from them
remains in the possession of my friend the
Antiquary himself. It would be impossible
to imagine a task more congenial, for a man
of his special tastes and culture, than this
great labor of exploring a buried city of the
mysterious Gaulish time, and his perseverance
has been fully rewarded. The diggings of
each year, in consequence of an agreement
with the owner of the property, have to be
filled up with earth again in the autumn, so
that the casual visitor, especially if he comes
early in the summer, inevitably receives an
impression that very little has been done. But
he who has followed the work year by year, as
I have, can well understand how attractive it
must be to a thoroughly accomplished antiquary, who pursues it with a clear knowledge
of what the soil has yielded, and may be expected still to yield. At first, when I heard,
after a particularly successful season, that all
the buildings were to be buried again after
their temporary disinterment, it seemed to
me a lamentable necessity ; but the Antiquary
soon convinced me that the interests of knowl-

edge and those of the owner of the land were
identical in this, for the reinterment of the
buildings was the only sure guaranty of their
preservation for a distant future.   Even the
effect of the weather upon the uncemented
Gaulish walls — for the Gauls only used clay
for mortar — would in a few years reduce
their houses to mere indistinguishable heaps,
whilst all the hewn stones of the later Roman
dwellings would certainly be carried away by
the peasants, if left exposed to their unhis-
torical feelings of admiration.

The life on the Mount has quite a peculiar
charm for me, which I would convey to the
reader if it were only possible.   There is a
constant interest in the excavations, for almost
every hour brings something curious to light,
and if we are absent for a day there is sure to
be a small collection of curiosities awaiting
our return in the evening.   It is impossible
to imagine a more agreeable host than my
friend the Antiquary, and it would be difficult
perhaps to find a guest more easily satisfied, as
for luxuries, than I am ; indeed, to confess the
truth, the very roughness and simplicity of
our existence on the Mount are profoundly
agreeable to my feelings, just as a rough towel

is agreeable to my skin. The sort of refine-
ment which is represented by carpets and
French polish is in my opinion rather irritating than agreeable, and if a certain yachtsman
whose cabin is furnished in blue and white
satin were to make me a present of his craft,
no feelings of gratitude would be strong
enough to make me endure such upholstery a
day. On the Mount we have no such imped-
iments to true comfort, and I am happy to
say, too, that Pauchard is not one of those
terrible French cooks who serve three times
as many dishes as an Englishman requires.
He gives us enough, but not too much, which
is the perfect art of making dinner agreeable.
The very things upon the table belong to the
place, and are in keeping with the purpose of
the Antiquary's sojourn here. The water jugs
and wine bottles are set upon fragments of
Gaulish pottery by way of table mats, and
when we eat boiled eggs our egg cups are
broken necks of amphoræ. The chimney-
piece is made of three stones taken from a
Gaulish house, and the latest chisel-mark upon
them is anterior to the time of Cæsar. The
side pieces are great slabs of granite, but the
entablature is a thick piece of white stone

with two sockets sunk in it at a little distance from the ends. It was the sacred white threshold stone of the Gaulish dwelling, and those two sockets were made to receive the upright posts of wood. Although we are in June, and a Burgundy June, my host has a great fire in the chimney every evening to remove any remains of winter damp that may linger about the room. Firewood is a luxury of which the supply is practically unlimited on the Beuvray, for we are surrounded by the dense forest, and whenever the weather is chilly, as it often is at that height in the evening, we make fires that would astonish a Parisian. When the strange rude chimney is filled with blazing logs, and lighted by their glare, it looks like a Druid temple illuminated by the flames of a sacrifice.

The walls of the room, as I said, are covered with rough mortar, yet artists and scholars who have visited the place have amused their leisure in covering them with sketches and inscriptions.

The master of the house has himself written above the chimney-piece, in large Greek letters,

'ΕΙΡΗ´ΝΗ,

which is his way of saying " Pax vobiscum "
to his guests; and truly here is peace, the
peace of loving kindness and good will,
the peace, too, of beautiful nature, far from
the noise of cities.

Another wall is entirely covered with
mediæval tapestry, a forest scene with quaintly
costumed figures. This is the only luxury
about the place, but it is not Philistine luxury,
— Philistinism would have begun by putting
the tapestry on the floor, had it possessed such
a thing. Those strange figures and that dark
green foliage glimmer mysteriously in the
glow of the firelight, and we feel that they are
with us when scarcely looking at them directly.
It suits the Antiquary's comprehensive interest
in the past to have the middle ages represented
here along with times of far higher antiquity.

His too great indulgence has permitted a
good deal of rough sketching on the other
walls. For example, there is a big charcoal
drawing, of which I am *not* the author, representing my arrival here,

> " Once upon a midnight dreary,"

with two companions and my faithful Cocotte,
who is turned into a sumpter horse for the
occasion, and laden with all our baggage.

The artist has rather abused his permission
to blacken the wall with charcoal, but to
relieve the general blackness he has taken
the liberty, or rather license, of introducing a
moon that was not visible at all when the incident happened.   This may, however, be permitted to him as a compensation for what lay
entirely beyond his power, and was therefore
of necessity omitted.   The fact is, that as on
that occasion we arrived very late, — that is to
say, at one o'clock in the morning, — the Antiquary was asleep in one of the wooden huts,
and Pauchard was asleep in the other. I had
foreseen this and planned nothing less than a
serenade, which we practised diligently in the
wood till we could sing it tolerably in tune.
The serenade I chose for the occasion is an exceedingly beautiful one : the music is perfect
serenader's music, with the true poetical pas-
sionate rising and falling of the voice, like the
sighing of the wind, and to hear it well sung
in the South of France, as I first heard it,
with a guitar, carries you to Granada and the
Alhambra at once and plunges you in a dream
of passion, moonlight, and a balcony.   It was
certainly the first time in his life that the Antiquary had been addressed as a charming girl of

Granada. However, we managed to keep grave enough to sing our parts in tune, and sang with great strength in the *fortissimos* to awaken the sleeper, and equal softness in the *pianissimos* to soothe him again : —

> " Charmante fille de Grenade,
> À mes accents réveille toi!
> N'entends-tu pas la sérénade?
> C'est moi, c'est moi, c'est moi!
> Oui! c'est moi, ton amant fidèle,
> Ton Lorenzo, qui chante ici,
> Mais tu parais, ma toute belle.
> Merci ! Merci !
> Tra la *la*, tra la la la la *la*, tra la la la la *la*,
> la la *la*, la la *la*," etc.

The Antiquary first began to dream he was at the Opera, then gradually awoke in the darkness of his hut; but the music, still persisting, produced the strangest effect upon his mind. "Am I still dreaming?" he thought, "or can there be really music like this in the wild woods of the Beuvray?" Then he opened the door of his hut and looked out upon us. Pauchard turned out, too, and prepared us a supper, after which we sat talking and smoking for an hour or two before going to bed, our good-natured host being perfectly delighted by his musical awakening. As for

Pauchard, he was most flattering in his eulo-
gium of our music, and prepared our supper
with the air of a man who was convinced that
we had fully deserved it.

It has happened to me more than once to
drop in upon the Antiquary quite unexpect-
edly in the late evening, when he was sitting
alone, writing the record of his discoveries. I
shall always pleasantly remember my first
visit to the Mount, on foot, with a knapsack
and staff, alone. It was late twilight when
I got to the summit, and the difficulty was
to find the Antiquary's hut, for his encampment consisted of a single hut at that time,
but by a strange mixture of reasoning and
good luck I went straight to the nook where
it lay hidden. Much of the happiness of the
old camp in the Highlands came back to me
that evening, and the solitary hut on the hill-
top surrounded by vast forests, with loaded
revolvers hanging on the walls, had a romantic
interest that the cottage will never rival.
Besides, I believed then in the solitude of
the Beuvray, but have since discovered that
there is no place in the neighborhood where
you are less likely to enjoy a day of privacy.
However, we have it to ourselves at night.

CHAPTER IV.

HOW firmly and insensibly particular customs establish themselves in particular
situations! The Antiquary and I have a fixed
habit of taking a walk on the summit of the
Mount at midnight. We never made a rule
of this consciously, but the habit has formed
itself from circumstances. We sit talking
after dinner till it is near midnight, and then
the cottage has to be arranged as a bedroom
for one of us; so, whilst Pauchard is busy with
this work, we leave the field clear for him, and
go out. The cottage is within a hundred
yards of the summit, and the night air that

blows over it is cool and refreshing. Few places that I have ever visited are so impressive as the Mount at midnight. The ground on the top is nearly flat for the space of two or three acres, and the table-land is luckily almost clear of trees except a few glorious beeches that have crowned it for a thousand years. The sides slope down precipitously so that their thick woods do not impede the view, for the tops of the trees are below us. The vast prospect, extending when the air is clear from Mont Blanc to the Loire, is vague and misty under the moonlight, but we can make out some of the details nevertheless, as you can in a Turner landscape; we can recognize the tower-capped height of Touleur, the castled crag of La Roche Millay, lofty themselves, yet a thousand feet below us, and we can at least determine the situation of many a hamlet and village that lie shrouded by the valley mist. Our geography is greatly aided by two small lakes, for water is always recognizable even in misty moonlight, and we can see these lakes quite plainly when all the earth seems scarcely more definite or substantial than an exhalation. One night it occurred to me that, from the situation of the moon, she would appear

reflected in one of these lakes from a certain
point upon the hill, so I took the Antiquary
there, and we beheld for the first and only
time one of the most singular effects imagi-
nable. Absolutely nothing on the earth was
visible except that distant lake. It was
rippled by a light breeze, and the surface,
catching the moon's reflection, appeared like
a sheet of golden fire in an unfathomable
abyss of space.

On the little plateau of the Beuvray there
is the site of an ancient temple, which I examined in detail when it was laid bare in the
course of the excavations, and within the
foundations of this temple stood, in a later
age, the walls of a little Christian church, with
the round apse of the Romanesque architecture. Then the church disappeared, and a
chapel or oratory was built at the east end of
it, dedicated to Saint Martin. Afterwards
the oratory also disappeared, and now the
Antiquary is building a new one exactly
within the apse of the Christian Church. He
and his architect have spared no effort to
make this little structure as permanent as
human work can ever be. It is built entirely
of large blocks of granite, and not only the

walls, but also the roof and the floor, are of
this enduring material. The architecture is
very simple, Romanesque in principle but
without any ornament whatever, and the whole
structure consists of nothing but a small apse,
a tiny space representing the choir before the
apse, and an open porch as wide as the whole
edifice, with an arch supported by simple
square pillars. The altar is to be very simple
also, a slab of massive stone, and the candle-
sticks will be of substantial iron, fixed in their
place in the stone. Over the altar there is to
be a stone altar-piece representing a legend
about Saint Martin, which the reader may
never have heard. The legend says that
Christ in Heaven appeared once with a poor
tattered garment that covered half his person,
when an Apostle asked the reason, and Christ
answered, " Martin hath clothed me so," for
Martin had given half his garment to one of
Christ's poor on earth. There is already a
substantial cross of granite not far from the
new oratory, and on the pedestal of the cross
is a small bas-relief representing the entry of
Saint Martin into Amiens, where also he performed a famous act of charity. So far as
anything can be accepted as historical in the

life of so famous a saint, it does appear certain that he preached in these parts and on this spot. For, solitary as may be the summit of the Beuvray at midnight, and high as it is above the level of the surrounding country, the place has been frequented by multitudes, on certain occasions, ever since the old Gaulish times, when a multitude lived there permanently.

Every year, down to the present year, a fair has been held here on the first Wednesday in May from the Pagan days, when the merchants came to sacrifice to Maia, and to Mercury her son, so that the month was Maia's month, and the day was Mercury's day. And if we could only witness those successive first Wednesdays in May as they have been kept on the summit of the Beuvray for the last two thousand years, we should witness the slow transitions of humanity from those ancient times to ours, we should watch the gradual change of costume and of usage, we should hear the change of speech. But if I might not witness the slow vicissitudes of two thousand Mays gone by, if I might choose one May only amongst them all, my choice would soon be fixed. I would have it in the middle ages

at the time when they held a tournament here
on the hilltop, and the great Baron of La
Roche Millay rode up from his castle, clothed
in complete steel, and met here many a proud
count and baron, each with his train of vas-
sals. Of all places in the world to choose for
a tournament, the crest of a mountain is the
most singular and the most romantic. It is
like the meeting of ghostly warriors in the
clouds, and it does not require any great
stretch of imagination, when one is alone on
this crest at midnight, under the dim light of
a waning moon, to fancy the knights in armor
careering over their old tournament ground
once more, and then leaping over the pre-
cipitous edge to vanish in misty air. The
peasantry of the neighboring villages have
preserved a memory of shadowy horsemen in
their superstitions, and few are the peasants
who would care or dare to accompany us in
our midnight ramble over this haunted ground.

But their traditions seem rather to point
to the times of Roman warfare than of Gothic
feast and tournament. They tell you of a
white horse that gallops over the hill's crest
at midnight, and of a loud voice commanding
ghostly legions in Latin. Now when you

reflect that these villagers have no historical
literature whatever, nothing but oral traditions
from one generation to another, does it not
seem rather wonderful that they should have
preserved this memory of the Roman invasion?
They have also kept a certain number of Latin
words of command. I know that one of them,
on meeting an animal in the night that fright-
ened him, exclaimed, "*Horror! Terror!*"—
pure Latin as one could wish, — and it appears
that he regarded these words as a species of
exorcism, yet they are not words of Catholic
exorcism certainly, but an exclamation of fear
and astonishment natural enough in a Roman.
Strangely enough that superstition about the
white horse of the Beuvray, which has made
many a rustic quake with fear when belated
upon the hill, has been confirmed of late, to
the eye at least, if not to the critical intelligence. A white horse *has* often been seen
both by Pauchard and the Antiquary, but,
unfortunately for the effect of their testimony,
I am bound to add that it was a living one.

The phantom war-horse and loud-voiced
Latin-speaking phantom commander are not,
however, the only ghosts that haunt the Mount
and the forest. In the middle ages there dwelt

a certain seigneur in the castle whose ruins are
still visible on the rocky peak of Touleur, and
his custom was to hunt over the Beuvray
with his dogs. He hunts there still, in the
night-time, and still the peasants affirm that
the cry of his dogs and the sound of his horn
and voice may be heard above the noise of
the winds. So seriously and earnestly do they
believe this, that a gamekeeper at La Roche
Millay, perfectly well known to the Antiquary,
has gone night after night over the mountain
in order to catch a glimpse of the phantom
hunter and his hounds ; but he says, quite
gravely, that although he has heard them
many a time, and walked after them many a
league, he has never yet been able to get a
glimpse of them. Evidently this must be a
version of the well known Northern superstition of the *Gabriel Ratchets*, or *Gabble Raches*,
but in this instance firmly localized by attach-
ing it to the name of a definite baron hunting
over a definite hunting-ground. The Gabriel
Ratchets are phantoms that hunt in the air,
and pass over your head in the late evening
or night, when you hear, but never can see
them ; and the origin of this superstition is
supposed to be simply the flight of large mi-

gratory birds, — wild swans, perhaps, or geese.
The phantom hunter of Touleur is, however,
believed to hunt on the ground, in the forest
of the Beuvray, and it is believed, too, that
any one who met him would see him and his
hounds, as if they were in the flesh. The
romance of this legend is in this instance
greatly heightened by the romantic scenery
where it is placed. The ruined castle of Touleur is perched upon the summit of a beautiful wooded hill with a rocky crest, between
which and the Beuvray lies a valley of well
watered pastures, and the side of the Beuvray
which is opposite Touleur is hollowed into a
deep gorge by which the ghostly hunter must
ascend. There is a legend, too, that Saint
Martin leaped over this wide and deep ravine
of Malvaux on his donkey, and arrived on a
hard rock which was indented by the donkey's
hoofs when it descended. The peasants believe this sincerely, and show the ass's hoof-
mark on the rock. Of course there is a
reason for this extraordinary feat. In the year
376, the saint came to the Beuvray to preach
against the Pagan worship which was still celebrated there, and overthrew the altars of the
ancient gods ; but when the deed was accom-

plished the incensed Pagans were still strong enough to put the saint to flight, and his ass took this miraculous leap to save him. The Christian traditions of the Beuvray do not end here, for in the fourteenth century a monastery was built on the opposite slope of the Mount, and fortified. The place, however, cannot have been sufficiently strong to resist a military force, and was probably only fortified against brigands, for it was sacked and burnt in 1570 by an army of Calvinists, in their passage from Autun to Moulins-Engilbert, and so little remains of it at the present day that it would be difficult even to make out the plan of its foundations without excavating.

There is one acknowledged evil in our life upon the Mount,— an evil which it would be easy to remedy, yet which circumstances appear to impose upon us, — and that is insufficiency of sleep. Although perfectly masters of our own time, the Antiquary and I, by an illogical combination of a bad habit with a good one, so manage matters that we do not get sleep enough for the wants of our bodily constitutions. It is generally half-past one in the morning when we return from our midnight walk, which is the bad habit, — and we get up early, which is the good habit, — but the two go badly together and after a few days of it we begin to look dreamy in the daytime, and to have that strange feeling of unreality which insufficiency of sleep produces. I well remember, on one occasion, going to bed at three in the morning and getting up to wash in cold spring water and see the Mont Blanc at five. The cold water we are always sure of, but we are not always so sure of Mont Blanc; sometimes, however, the range of his *aiguilles* is clearly visible at sunrise, and occasionally but more rarely at sunset, when it is going to rain. *The distance is a hundred and fifty-seven miles as the crow flies.* To realize the full marvel of this, let the reader transfer the same distance to the map of England. It is the distance from London to Scarborough. Imagine a mass of rock at Scarborough big enough to be visible from London, and you have an accurate measure of this marvellous extent of prospect.

It is rather the fashion to laugh at views from mountains at sunrise, because tourists climb a hill occasionally, and find themselves surrounded by dense mists; but the tradition

that sunrise is worth seeing from a high mountain is perfectly well founded, for this is one
of the grandest spectacles on the earth. We
have quite a habit of watching it from the
Beuvray, which accounts for our early rising.
I think an informed mind realizes the full
grandeur of the planetary motion better on
these occasions than on any other, and to my
feeling the knowledge of that sublime reality
is incomparably more impressive than the
most imaginative dreams of ancient faith or
poetry. To believe that Apollo is driving the
solar chariot westward in the heavens does not
tax our powers so much as the far vaster conception that the whole of the human race is
carried eastward to the sunshine by the regular, unfailing motion of the globe that we
inhabit. How small from the top of even a
little mountain do men and their labors
appear upon the earth, and how even a little
lifting above their level enables us to think
more easily of the globe as a huge material
thing that exists independently of the prodigious masses of life which it sustains! It is
only in rare moments, but more frequently on
mountain tops than elsewhere, that we think
of the earth's mass in any conscious way what-

ever; but on the Beuvray, with such a mountain as Mont Blanc clear with its serrated
sharp edge against the eastern sky, and such
a river as the Loire gleaming in the western
plain through which it flows to the far Atlantic,
it is inevitable that our ideas should become
vaster if we would grasp the full significance
of the scene. How grand is the silence of
the mountains when the night shadow is still
resting on the plain, and only the crests are
caught by the first golden light of the morning! Cool breezes blow through the foliage
of the ancient beech trees, and there is a
delightful freshness in this clear, high atmosphere that we shall lose when the sun grows
hot.

CHAPTER V.

IF we were inclined to go to sleep on our return to the cottage, there would be a difficulty due to the industrious alacrity of Pauchard. Beds have disappeared, windows and doors are open for ventilation, the board on trestles is re-established, and a hospitable board it is. Then come two great basins of capital soup, for Pauchard only makes one kind of soup, except on Fridays, and by long practice he makes that one kind inimitably well. Our days on the Beuvray are not spent in lolling on the grass by the cool fountains

under the shady trees, so we need a good
preparation for our toils, and we are both
agreed that soup is practically the best because
it conveys most nourishment into the system
at least cost to the digestive powers. After
the soup, which contains a substantial quantity
of bread and vegetables, the Antiquary gives
directions to his servant, and we sally forth for
our morning walk. My friend is a terrible
pedestrian, and it is necessary to be rather
cautious in setting out with him. "Let us
take a little turn," he says, and if you follow
without settling on some fixed route he will
lead you over the most fatiguing and imprac-
ticable ground for a dozen miles without
thinking about it, after which, if you venture
on any inquiry or remonstrance, he will turn
round with the most innocent, surprised look,
and say, "*Mais, vous n'êtes pas fatigué?*" If
from pride or vanity you say you are not
tired, he will go on quite indefinitely, but
if you frankly confess that you have enough
of it, then he will only lead you back by a
worse and still more circuitous route than that
you have already traversed, in order to show
you the country, or some stone or mound
which he considers interesting from the anti-

quarian point of view. He is little and thin, and sixty years old, but one of the best pedestrians I ever met with, especially on rough ground. I am put at a disadvantage with him in one respect: he can bear heat like an ostrich, and just when the sun flames in all his fury my friend feels lightest and most youthful, whereas my Northern temperament has an objection to being roasted. With a companion his walks are generally moderate, because the companion is a drag, but by himself, in perfect liberty, without any restraint whatever, he goes wonderful distances. For example, I know that he set out one morning from his own house with the simple purpose of taking a little walk, and came back quietly to dinner. When asked where he had been, he mentioned half a dozen villages. "And did you never make use of any kind of conveyance?" He answered simply that he had been on foot the whole time, and yet to visit the villages he mentioned implied a walk of forty miles.

A thorough exploration of the Mount is a very hard day's work indeed, and visitors who come here to picnic learn very little about it. There are twenty miles of Gaulish roads in

the woods, and a good many other miles of
walking along ancient ramparts and from one
interesting point to another. In moderate
walks, still rather fatiguing from the steepness
of the ground, it takes about a week to see
everything that has either antiquarian or artistic interest. Nothing can be more agreeable
than these rambles when too much is not
crowded into each day, and the true charm of
so charming a place is not to be realized at
once, but grows upon the mind gradually by
habit and acquaintance. To know the place
properly, one ought to begin with a careful
study of the ramparts, and this is not easy, for
where most interesting and best preserved
they are often buried in the dense forest. In
their greatest size and perfection they reminded me very much of a railway embankment on the side of a steep hill, being quite
as large, with a road on the top, too hard for
trees to take root in ; covered with short grass,
in other parts of the circumference the ramparts were of much less importance, but always
quite distinctly traceable. Where best preserved there are two roads, one on the top of
the earthwork and the other running parallel
to it at the base. Just on the crest of the

Mount there is also an inner fortification on the west side, where the ground is not nearly so steep as on the eastern. These interior earthworks probably defended a citadel; they are in good preservation, but do not, when excavated, present any traces of the woodwork which was so important a part of the outer rampart, or true wall of the city. The structure of this Gaulish wall is one of the most interesting things about the place, but to understand it thoroughly it is almost essential to have been present, as I was, when a portion of the wall itself was carefully dissected with pickaxe and spade. About four hundred yards of wall, including one of the entrances to the city, were studiously anatomized in this manner, and found to answer accurately to Cæsar's description of Avaricum, in the Seventh Book *De Bello Gallico.* I will translate the passage here : —

"This is generally the form of all Gaulish walls. Straight beams all in one length are placed upon the ground at equal distances of two feet; these are placed inside the wall and covered with a good deal of earth. But these intervals which we have mentioned are faced with large stones. These having been placed and fastened together, another course is superadded, the same interval being preserved, nor do the beams ever touch each other, but, being separated by equal spaces, each several range of beams is closely sustained with a course of stones between. The whole of the work is thus successively woven together, until the regular height of the rampart is attained. On the one hand this sort of work has not a bad appearance with its variety of alternate beams and stones which keep their ranks with straight lines; on the other hand it is most advantageous for the defence of cities, since the stone protects it from fire and the wood against the battering-ram, the wood being fixed within the beams, generally forty feet long, and is not to be either penetrated or disjointed."

These walls have been very fully described and illustrated in the Life of Cæsar by Napoleon III. Cæsar's description is clear so far as its brevity permits, yet not quite perfectly clear. The long beams were parallel with the course of the wall and were inside it, then there were upright pieces and cross-pieces, which were fastened by large iron nails to the long beams. This presented a series of rude panels, which were backed in the interior with earth, but outwardly faced with substantial stone, so that the wooden framework remained visible, but the stone facing was flush with it, as a

builder would say. It follows, therefore, that
in excavating this wall the Antiquary might
expect to find traces of the woodwork that
had formed part of it, and also the large iron
nails that fastened the beams together. I
happened to be present some years ago during
this very interesting part of the excavations,
and everything we found confirmed what was
already known of this peculiar system of construction. We found stonework still existing
to the height of a yard, and the empty places
of the wooden uprights with carbonized wood
always at the bottom of them, and these *trous
der poutres*, as the Antiquary called them, were
at such regular distances that he could easily,
by measurement, predict where they would be
found. The upright stanchions had been fixed
in the hardened earth, but the matter was quite
soft in the holes where they had been fixed, so
that, by a simple process of removing stones
and soil, the holes became visible at once in
their regular order. The Antiquary expected
to find the huge nails which had fastened the
cross-pieces, and in that he was not disap-
pointed, for the nails were still sticking upright in their original position, though the
wood had decayed around them. I have said

that the part of the wall explored included one of the gates of the city. This was of peculiar interest, having been defended with especial care.

The wall was turned inwards by two elbows, so that there was a narrow lobby or passage to be got through before the enemy could reach the interior. Considerable quantities of burnt wood were found near the gateway, which the Antiquary attributes to the burning of wooden towers placed to defend the entrance. A ditch twelve yards wide by five deep was rich in such things as coins, bracelets, ornaments in polished stone, broken hand-mills, and vases.

Not very far from the entrance, and just by the roadside within the wall, the Antiquary was lucky enough to come upon a Gaulish blacksmith's shop, with abundant evidence of the sort of labor performed there, and not much farther he found a shop that had been occupied by a workman of a higher grade, an enameller, with many fragments of enamelled work that did credit to the skill of an age that is too commonly believed to have been in a state of savagery. I remember the day when, to our great delight, we actually found part of the enameller's bellows, the tube of which had been made of enduring earthen-ware. Many of the Gaulish houses were in a remarkably good state of preservation, the walls being still high, and the floors so very hard that the workmen broke their pickaxes upon them. The system of construction with upright oak stanchions had been followed a good deal in the city as well as the rampart, and the hard floors often presented soft places at regular intervals that were the stanchion-holes with carbonized wood in them. The number of *amphoræ* found in these places was wonderful. I remember how a single laborer discovered thirty or forty of them in one spot, all lying close together. The houses were much more crowded than they are in a modern city, and if the reader thinks of them as clusters of cellars with thatched roofs, and entrance through the roofs by ladders, he will not be far wrong for a great many of them. There were some better dwellings, but chiefly of the Roman time. One very large mansion was discovered quite close to the Antiquary's own hut, and he little suspected when erecting that humble dwelling that he had chosen for the site of it the Belgravia of the ancient city.

This mansion had many chambers and a large bathroom with a great bath in perfect condition, built of fine stones as well dressed as they could be. A good sewer passed near to the house, — not a mere drain, but a sewer big enough for a man to walk in, — and there were some remnants of fluted columns. During all these diggings the usual quantity of small objects were found from week to week, and these in the course of the eight years that have already passed would have filled a little museum of themselves. Every ancient dwelling has been systematically measured, and drawn to scale on a plan of the whole city.

Now the question is, What was the ancient name of this Gaulish city, and what was its place in history? Did Cæsar ever visit it?

A great controversy on this question has raged for many a year, and if I were to go into the details of this controversy I should easily fill a volume with the arguments on each side. It must be treated very summarily in this place. My friend the Antiquary firmly believes the city to be the ancient Bibracte, which gives intense offence to many inhabitants of Autun who consider that he is robbing their town of its claim to prehistoric antiquity,

for Autun has hitherto very generally been
assured to be the Bibracte of Cæsar and
Strabo.   However, my friend is neither the
first nor the only one to hold this opinion
about Bibracte.   There was a certain juris-
consult of the sixteenth century named Guy
Coquille, who wrote upon the customs of the
Nivernais, and quite decidedly fixed Bibracte
on the Beuvray.   He settled the question in
twenty lines.   In the next century, the matter was taken up by Adrien de Valois, a
geographer who advocated the same opinion;
then came a writer called D'Anville in the
seventeenth century, who began by agreeing
with De Valois, but not having material
enough for evidence, as no excavations were
made at that time, fell back upon Autun as
the most probable site of Bibracte; and after
him the question was held to be quite in
favor of Autun, so that nobody argued any
more upon the subject, which fell into "the
deep slumber of decided opinion."   This
silence reigned until the year 1856, when my
friend the Antiquary took it up again.   His
first view was simply the opinion generally
received, and, like most other inhabitants of
Autun, he knew nothing about the Beuvray;

but being engaged at that time upon a work on the defensive system of the Romans,[1] he heard from the peasants that there were curious ramparts upon the Beuvray, so he went and really looked at them. After the visit he returned home, convinced that he was in presence of a great archæological problem, and proposed to the *Société Eduenne* the idea of making an accurate map of these fortifications, which was executed accordingly. I may just observe, by way of parenthesis, that the Antiquary's powers of pedestrianism went for a good deal in his rediscovery of Bibracte; for if he had been as idle as many of his countrymen are he would not have taken the trouble to go round the ramparts, a thing his critics never do for any consideration.

When once this idea, " This must be Bibracte," had taken root in the Antiquary's mind, it naturally gathered to itself many facts and observations, as a theory always does, this being the advantage of holding a theory, especially when the validity of it is generally denied. On re-reading Strabo the Antiquary found that he called Chalon a πόλις and Bibracte a

[1] Système défensif des Romains dans le pays Eduen. 1856.

φρούριον, which sometimes especially means
a hill fort, and always implies *fortress* more
than πόλις does. Cæsar called Bibracte an
"oppidum longe maximum æque copiosissi-
mum." The length of the ramparts answers
to the first half of this description, and the
productive wealth of the neighboring country
to the second. With reference to Cæsar's
descriptive talent I here permit myself the
liberty of a little outspoken criticism. He
has been immensely praised, and over-praised,
as a writer. It is possible that, considered
simply as a narrator of military events, he
may excel in clearness and simplicity, but he
was a singularly poor literary artist. His
mind appears to have been entirely filled up
with figures (numbers of men and horses), distances, and *names*, and he was so bad a traveller as to suppose that names were enough,
forgetting that they have a meaning only
just so far as the reader is already aware what
is meant by them. For example, if in writing
a book to be read in England and in America
I use the name " Paris " without explanation,
it is well, because everybody knows what sort
of a place Paris is, but if I use the name
" Montmoret " I ought to explain clearly what

sort of a place Montmoret is the first time I use the word — after that the word may stand alone. Now, suppose that in this book, for instance, the word *Montmoret* were to occur several times without explanation, the reader would have a fair right to complain that the author did not understand his business. Well, this is just what may be said of Cæsar, as to his writing — not as to his generalship. He contented himself with a name, and yet without asking from any ancient writer such detailed description as is common in modern works, in which there is often too much of it; we certainly have a right to complain that when a single sentence would have contained all the information that posterity asks for, Cæsar, who could so easily have given it, is silent. No two sites for a city can be more different than Autun and the crest of the Beuvray. Autun is on a rising ground between a river and a range of hills, divided from the hills by a valley; the Beuvray is a great isolated mount at least twelve miles from the river. If the site of Bibracte was the site of Autun, Cæsar might surely have mentioned the river; and if on the other hand Bibracte was on the Beuvray, he might have

mentioned the hill.   One can hardly imagine
a modern traveller — any Livingstone, Speke,
or Palgrave — describing the country in a
manner so careless of the reader's legitimate
curiosity.   Cæsar seems to have taken little
interest in physical geography, and to have
been entirely absorbed in his professional
business as a soldier. Yet if we consider
him simply as a military writer, we may
reasonably complain of his laconism even in
that limited capacity.   Rivers and mountains
are facts of military importance, besides being
interesting to landscape painters.   Imagine,
for example, a modern military writer telling
of the campaign in Abyssinia and forgetting
to say that Magdala was on a hill, or of the
campaign in the Ashantee country without
mentioning its rivers!   Here we feel the
utility of the modern war-correspondent, and
we regret that the chronological difficulty
should have made it impossible for Cæsar to
be accompanied by a clever professional writer
for the *Daily News*.   We should have known
all about Bibracte then.   As it is, we have
little in Cæsar to except the distance of
Bibracte from a battle-field; but as he did
not describe the battle-field either, the con-

troversialists on opposite sides put it in different places, so as to be at the proper distance from what they suppose to have been Bibracte. If Cæsar had been a good topographer, antiquaries would have lost many of the pleasures of debate, and my friend the Antiquary would probably have had nothing to discover.

CHAPTER VI.

CURIOUSLY enough, whilst the Antiquary was making his intentional excavations on the Beuvray, a railway company, without archæological intentions, was doing work of much archæological interest at Autun, and of a kind directly affecting this very question about the situation of Bibracte. A cutting for the line from Autun to Gantenay traversed Autun in its whole breadth, and down to a depth of six feet below the most ancient vestiges of human habitation. No trace of man's labors was found below the streets laid out by Augustus, which are in straight lines,

as regular as a chess-board, forming exact
squares of one hundred and seven metres on
every side. This extreme regularity of the
Roman town, like that of some new American
city erected on vacant ground, is considered
to be presumptive evidence that no Gaulish
city existed on the spot when Augustus laid
out his streets; yet even if such a city had
been demolished to make room for a new
one, it is still presumable that some fragments
of it would have remained below the surface,
so that excavation would have revealed Gaulish work at Autun as it has done on the
Beuvray; yet nothing more ancient than
Roman work has ever been found at Autun,
beneath the Roman ways, and there has
never been any material evidence that the
Augustan city was erected on ground pre-
viously occupied.

The history of the present archæological
excavations on Mount Beuvray is briefly as
follows. Before the year 1857 some work of
this kind had been begun by M. Xavier-de-
Garennes, who had written a book about the
Mount. After him, the owner of the property
— Viscount d'Aboville, whose name may be
familiar to the English reader as one of the

most extreme Legitimists in the National
Assembly — began to excavate on the summit. These excavations were under the direction of M. Bulliot, who is identical with the
Antiquary of these pages. Whilst he was
busy directing M. d'Aboville's excavations
the late Archbishop of Rheims, an old friend
of his, came to see. The Archbishop was a
man of more than commonly clear intelligence, and candid enough to acknowledge a
mistake. He had translated the orations of
the Athenian Eumenes, and in his notes to
these had found occasion to mention the
Beuvray, and to prove satisfactorily to himself that the notion of putting Bibracte there
was an insult to common sense; but when he
had seen the place and the small beginning
of excavation which had been accomplished
at that time, his opinion altered. The Archbishop dined with Napoleon III. at the camp
of Châlons, and told him what he had seen,
urgently recommending him to undertake
diggings in order to settle the question for
the Life of Cæsar. Then my friend the
Antiquary got a letter from the Emperor,
inviting him to an audience, went to the
Tuileries with a map of the Mount in his

pocket, and explained to his Majesty all that was already known. Napoleon took a great interest in the subject, and immediately became a convert to the Antiquary's opinion, which he expressed as his own in the Life of Cæsar; but a more important practical consequence of this interview was that the Emperor undertook excavations at his private expense and confided the direction of them to the Antiquary. His subsidy was not very large, but it was continued year after year; and as every franc of it was used with judgment, the results were very considerable. It has since been continued by the Minister of Public Instruction. This assistance from the Government accounts for the transfer of all portable finds to the Museum of St. Germains.

Eight long summers have now been spent in this work with the steadiness and regularity of a lucrative business, and in the face of much local ridicule and animosity. The Antiquary has many qualities that I respect very heartily indeed, but I respect none of them more than his persistent moral courage. Every one who knows what the provincial spirit is, and how immediately it fastens its slander and spite upon any labors above the

dead level of commonplace Philistine existence, will be prepared to hear that a man
who spent his summers in a hut on a hill-top
to dig for Gaulish antiquities immediately became the object of Philistine ridicule in his
own neighborhood.   The most wonderful
thing in this spirit is that it takes such strong
possession of minds that never concerned
themselves with the subjects under discussion.
It is intelligible, though to be regretted, that
one antiquary should speak bitterly of the
labors of another; but is it not astonishing
that people who never in their lives read a
line of any ancient author should be bitterer
still on subjects as much beyond their comprehension as the differential calculus?   Yet
the tongues of the most ignorant women
were excited to feverish activity against the
Antiquary, and they affirmed that he knew
nothing whatever of the subjects which had
occupied his leisure for twenty years, and
the whole of his time for ten.   I have
been perfectly amazed by the self-confidence
with which they settled his rank among the
savants.   I remember one lady especially who
affirmed that nothing whatever had been discovered upon the Beuvray except the remains

of the old convent, which everybody knew
about already. Other people admitted that
the Antiquary had found antiquities there,
but said that he had carried them up the hill
and had them buried to be disinterred whenever convenient in the presence of spectators
— I only hope that this theory was not intended to include the ramparts and the Gaulish houses. I have already mentioned the
condition on which these excavations have been
carried on, — the condition that they shall
always be filled up again in the autumn.
Hence when the Antiquary's enemies visit
the hill, which they do sometimes for a picnic
to see the view and have *déjeuner* on the top,
they can easily convince the ladies of the
party that nothing has been done. But by far
the most remarkable proof of bad faith in
some instances and intense prejudice in others
is what may be called the Great Water Argument. There is a strong and influential party
in Autun and the surrounding country who
base their convictions on the facts of nature.
They have certainly never read Professor
Huxley, but they profess adherence to the
spirit of his great words in praise of natural
knowledge when he said that men relied upon

the truths of science because they knew that
if they went to Nature, Nature would confirm
them. So it is urged that the Beuvray can
never have been inhabited by a numerous
population, because there is no water there.
This is one of the most perfect examples of
the strength of prejudice that I ever met with.
People of both sexes have said to me with
an air of triumphant satisfaction, " You know
there is one thing which proves conclusively
that there never can have been a city upon
the Beuvray, — there is no water, and that
settles the question." General Changarnier
belongs to this party; he says there is no
water on the Beuvray. Now the truth is
that there are no less than twenty-two per-
petual springs within the Gaulish ramparts,
some of which are very abundant; that three
rivulets flow down the sides of the hill; that
an antique well which I have seen was discovered on the very summit; and that the
water in this well, in the utmost heat of a
dry summer, was within eight feet of the
surface of the ground. Not only is it untrue
that the Mount is waterless like Etna, but the
truth is exactly the reverse of this. Mount
Beuvray is as remarkable for the inexhausti-

ble abundance of its waters and for the height
at which they spring as it is for their perfect
purity. So far from being deterred from
selecting this crest as the site of a great
oppidum because the garrison might suffer
from thirst, the Gauls would, on the contrary,
be attracted by the abundance of pure waters
that no enemy could divert from their city,
since the springs themselves were within the
circumference of its walls. Along the course
of one of the three brooks five artificial basins
were discovered during the excavations, with
a concrete bottom ten inches thick, evidence
enough that the inhabitants had paid attention to their water supply. Is not this Great
Water Argument a very pretty example of
the strength of prejudice? The controversy
about Bibracte has, however, produced mental
aberrations of a nature still more surprising.
The leader of the Autun party got into the
habit of writing bitter letters against the
Antiquary and addressing them to great personages, to the astonishment of the recipients;
and when I say great personages, I mean the
very greatest personages. The late Emperor
Napoleon often received these letters, but they
did not in the least affect his confidence in

the Antiquary.   Since the fall of the Empire
letters from the same source have reached the
Minister of Public Instruction for the time
being, and also certain foreign personages,
including no less a notability than Prince
Bismarck.   I happen to have read the letter
which was addressed to Bismarck, and I happen to know, on the best possible authority,
that *he* read the letter and had a hearty laugh
over it.   The Chancellor must have met with
many human curiosities, but it may well be
doubted whether he ever met with such a
specimen of the perfectly unscrupulous con-
troversialist as the author of that extraordinary
epistle.   Another letter by the same writer
formed the subject of conversation at an
august dinner-table where a great personage
appeared more puzzled by it than amused.

Although there is still much local hostility
against the Antiquary, his theory is now very
generally accepted by the learned world outside, and every year adds to the number of
his supporters.   The local hostility has disturbed him very little, and only served to
attach him more firmly to the work so well
begun.   A more trying infliction is that of
tourists who come for their amusement.   I

do not mean the learned tourist who can understand what he is told, but the ignorant fashionable tourist who wastes the Antiquary's time, intrudes upon his privacy, and is incapacitated by his own levity for any understanding of the Antiquary's explorations. Unfortunately, the huts and cottage are situated close to one of the Gaulish roads by which these people most easily ascend, and about eleven in the morning, our time for *déjeuner*, a whole company of them falls upon us at once. Nothing can be more disagreeable than these invasions. Some previous experience in Great Britain had quite prepared me for what we had to expect. If you happen to be living in a tent, or a hut, or a rude cottage, people who think themselves models of good manners will behave towards you with the most consummate indiscretion. They will open a tent curtain and peep in at you possibly just when you are undressed, they will crowd round the windows of a hut, they will open the door of a cottage and penetrate, uninvited, into the interior. They appear entirely to forget that your tent, hut, or cottage is just as much your mansion for the time being as their own

houses are theirs, and that an intrusion is just
as unpardonable in the one case as it would
be in the other. How the Antiquary endures
it seems almost past comprehension. In his
place I would have hedged round the camp
like Robinson Crusoe's citadel and put man-
traps and spring-guns, — at any cost I would
have had privacy *chez moi.* He had been
obliged to consider convenience of access for
himself, and therefore had to be near the
road, and the water question (so important for
camp or house) had fixed him near a fountain; but there were many other fountains to
choose from, and it would have been easy
to make a hundred yards of private road leading to a hidden citadel. A hundred yards,
in these cases, may make the difference between snug retirement and uncomfortable
publicity. I once encamped in Scotland
within that distance of a public road, in-
fested by tourists, and not one of them found
me out, thanks to a little mound of earth and
a few bushes. It was amusing to hear them
pass without a suspicion that my camp was
there, for they would not have passed so
readily if they had known of it.

One day the Antiquary and I, with a com-

mon friend of ours, were all happily at *déjeuner* in the cottage, when our happiness
was suddenly clouded by one of those appari-
tions that are much more inimical to peace
than the white horse or the phantom hunts-
man. Fifteen tourists came in a body. First
they looked in at us through the window, and
then they came inside and crowded the room
where we were eating. There was some
bacon hung up in a corner of the room with
the punning inscription, "l'Art pour tous,"
so one of the ladies inquired if we sold bacon.
It was of course simply impossible for Pauchard to continue the service of our table,
and our repast was suspended for about half
an hour. Our visitors were a distinguished
party of nobility, but my impression is that
when you go in a body to pay a visit to a
gentleman in any house or cottage that it
may please him to inhabit, you ought not to
crowd into his dining-room and interrupt his
meal so that his guests have to wait half an
hour between two dishes. At last, however,
they went out again and we resumed our
forks ; but suddenly the Antiquary said to
me, " I do hope you have locked your hut
(he had surrendered one of the huts to me

for a study and bedroom), for if you have not,
those people will be inside it, and I have a lot
of most precious things on the shelf which
they are likely enough to pilfer. You have
no notion how fashionable tourists will steal
when they have an opportunity." This reminded me that the shelves of my hut were
covered with a number of ancient ornaments
and curious specimens of the greatest value
as illustrations of the state of the arts in
Gaul, so I sprang from my seat and said,
" If any one is in the hut, he shall not be
in it long ! " Well, when I got there I found
a gentleman inside fingering the antiquities
in question, and a lady looking at the contents of my portmanteau, which lay open
on the bed. I turned both of them out
sharply, fastened the shutter inside, and then
locked the door in a sufficiently demonstra-
tive manner to make myself clearly understood. I hesitated an instant whether I
should not rather just turn the key on them,
leave them locked up together inside, and
set off to the woods for the rest of the day;
but consideration for the Antiquary's precious bits of Gaulish and Roman jewelry,
coins, etc., made me reflect that these people

were better outside the hut than in. It would have deeply gratified and amused me, however, to make prisoners of them, and I have ever since regretted that the precious antiquities ensured them liberty. The lady in question was a fashionable titled lady. It seemed, no doubt, perfectly natural to her to go into my bedroom and amuse herself by examining its contents; but suppose that I were to return the visit in the same manner? She lives at a great château, and I ask what impression would be produced in the noble society there if I were to penetrate, without permission, into *her* bedroom and examine the contents of her drawers? The answer is easy. I should most certainly be sent to prison. Then why does she consider herself authorized to do in my habitation what I might not do in hers? It is just possible that our plain, rough costume on the Mount,—for we wear nothing but old gray clothes there, and our big boots do not get blackened and polished like the boots of dandies on the boulevard,—with the rough walls of the cottage, its simple furniture and suspended flitch of bacon, may have inspired our visitors with the notion that we were not

persons worthy of much consideration; but
that is not a reason for invading our humble
dwellings.   It is strange, too, that the knowledge of good manners appears to be in in-
verse ratio to the rank of the personage.   I
thought it difficult to go beyond the indiscretion of the above-mentioned lady, but there
came two others of more elevated rank one
day who behaved still more inexcusably.
Their servant was sent up with provisions
for them, which he deposited at the cottage.
The weather was bad outside, and they came
to eat their luncheon in the Antiquary's simple room.   They behaved as if their bodies
were two icebergs, chilling the atmosphere,
and their souls two polar bears.   A young
gentleman present, a guest of the Antiquary,
and himself a scion of the most ancient nobility in France, was snubbed by them most
outrageously because he very kindly took the
trouble to be polite.   One of the two ladies
positively inquired " in what capacity (*à quel
titre*) the young man offered them these at-
tentions."   To which the Antiquary, who
is generally mildness itself, gave them an
answer which prevented any further observations of that nature.   The scene was at

the same time very irritating and very amusing. It would have delighted Thackeray, and
given him material for a chapter; it would
have disgusted Dickens, and converted anybody but a satirist into a democrat on the
spot. It is agreeable, however, to be able
to add that the Antiquary has pleasanter
visitors than these, even of high rank. The
Count of Paris came one day, studied everything conscientiously, and talked like a gentleman and a man of sense who had seen
the world. When great people have bad
manners it is often due to simple ignorance
of life. The late Emperor never found time
to visit the Mount personally, though the
place interested him greatly; but if he had
come and taken his *déjeuner* on the deal
board in the cottage, he would certainly have
left nothing but agreeable recollections of his
visit. With all his faults, he had delicacy
and tact, and the manners of a gentleman
with gentlemen. But then both the Count
and the Emperor had seen different classes of
society in other countries, and had not always
lived in the narrow life of a French château,
nor been absorbed in the contemplation of
their own immaculate nobility.

CHAPTER VII.

INDEPENDENTLY of the numbers of tourists who intrude uninvited on the Antiquary's privacy, his own hospitable disposition often crowds the little mountain establishment with friends, especially young friends. The tone that prevails there at these times is perfectly charming. A frank and lively gayety, with imperturbable good humor, reigns like steady sunshine over all, and there is an active willingness on the part of everybody to make things agreeable to everybody else. I had often been in societies where perfect dulness dwelt with perfect propriety, and sometimes in societies which were not dull, yet spoiled for thorough enjoyment by some defect of taste. I have rarely been with people who united so well good humor passing into extravagance, with an unfailing right sense of what is permissible and what is not. We were as merry for days together as if we had been as many profligates and prodigals, yet nothing was ever said that a young maiden might not have listened to.

The merriest person in the whole party was a young priest who a few weeks before had been one of the hostages condemned to death by the Commune. He was actually led forth to execution, and put in the same omnibus with the others who were to be shot that morning; but whilst they were in the street, the guard took pity on the youth of two passengers, and told them to go out and go their way. The transition from those terrible scenes and that imminence of violent death, to our free and joyous life on the Mount, put this young gentleman into such a state of happiness that it became perfectly exuberant, and the mere sight of his handsome, laughing face was as good as a glass of champagne. " You

must not imagine," the Antiquary said to me
one day when this youth had been making us
all laugh till our sides ached, "that he is in-
capable of serious thought, — on the contrary,
he is devoted to his profession ; but he is young
and healthy, and life is especially sweet to him
now, for the Shadow of Death has been upon
him." We had another young priest also in
the party, graver, but very cheerful, and he
and I took a liking for each other, and had
many a long talk together in quiet saunterings
under the ancient trees. Since then the first
of these two young men has devoted himself,
along with the companion who was saved at
the same time, entirely to the service of the
worst classes in great cities, and has chosen
for the scene of his labors one of the most disagreeable industrial towns in France. They
hope thus to do something towards the civilization of the Communards, and believe that
their own lives, so wonderfully rescued from
destruction, ought to be consecrated to the
good of their persecutors. My other young
friend of the Mount has taken vows of volun-
tary poverty and obedience, and is now a
teacher in a school, with arduous, monotonous
labor from day to day, from year to year, and

no pleasure, or liberty, or money.[1] Wide, indeed, are the differences of opinion between
these young men and me; but when I see
them thus, on the very threshold of manly
life, deliberately dedicating their entire ener-
gies to what they believe to be the best and
highest work that they can find to do in God's
service, I bow my head in unfeigned respect
for a resolve so earnest and so pure. Just
think of the almost incredible force of renun-
ciation that is needed for it! — the sacrifice of
family life, the abandonment of liberty, and
this without any compensating indulgence of
dreamy indolence, but with work from the
early morning, monotonous, and wearing, and
wearisome, and no wages in fame or gold, but
only the sense of an obscure utility, accepta-
ble in heaven! The Antiquary says that no
human strength of heart would be equal to it,
and he believes that a supernatural strength
is given. But whether you think with the
Antiquary that a Divine power is given specially in each individual case, or with me that

[1] This is to be taken in quite a literal sense. I mean that
my friend may not accept or possess any particle of the circu-
lating medium, not so much as a single coin of the lowest
value. He gets bare food and clothing.

such possibilities have been implanted in human nature at its origin, you are still in presence of a great sentiment carried out into strongly persistent practice, which is a spectacle more sublime than any we witnessed from the Mount, whether it were the pinnacles of the far Alps in the morning, or the broad Loire flowing away into the crimson flames of the sunset.

One day, when these and other young men were with us, the laborers made a great find, — they found a semicircular Gaulish fireplace in quite perfect preservation, with remains of charcoal in it from the last fire that the Gaul had burned there two thousand years ago upon Bibracte. This interested us all very much, and I proposed that we should kindle a fire once more on that antique hearth. Our young friends were delighted with this proposition, and so was the Antiquary; and when the shades of evening fell, and the stars were out, that ancient hearth was warmed once more, and it is an actual fact that the charcoal which had remained there cold and black since the Gaul quitted it was lighted again from our own firewood. There was not one of us who did not deeply feel the awful vastness of the interval between the last time that wood flamed there and the present. The entire space of time occupied by the history of Christianity had passed in the tremendous interval between the extinguishing and the rekindling of one of those bits of charcoal, the vast pageant of the Middle Ages with their countless wars, the slow formation of the mighty modern empires, the discovery and repeopling of America from the arctic solitudes to Cape Horn, the long genealogy of all the most ancient existing families in the world, the rise, decline, and fall of the Papacy as a temporal power, the whole history of royalty in France down to what may very probably have been its final extinction at Sedan, the grandeur of Spain, the grandeur of Holland, yes, even the grandeur of the Caliphs, — all had passed in that great gulf of time which the mind could not contemplate without giddiness. Of all these things we spoke, and I too, as an Englishman, had my special private thoughts about something that had passed between these two lightings of a fire. When the Gaul lighted his fire there the sons of Britain were powerless against the strength of Rome; but when we lighted our fire, Great Britain had become a

mother of nations and empress of subject
races, with a territory vaster than the dreams
of Cæsar and a population more numerous
than the multitudes of Alexander, whilst the
strength of every man in England had been
multiplied a hundred-fold by inventions never
imagined by any ancient, not even by the fer-
tile brain of Archimedes.

There are times in life which we remember
always, times which become a part of our conscious experience, to which we afterwards refer
as if they were dates of great events; yet these
times are often calm and uneventful. Our
evening by that Gaulish fireplace was one of
them. All who were present remember the
whole of that long evening vividly. We were
all in a condition of extreme sensitiveness to
romantic and poetic emotion, due to the
strangeness of the scene, to its perfect beauty,
and the entire absence of every discordant
element. We had all been strongly impressed
with the mere lighting of the fire, and the
warming of a hearth that had been cold since
the birth of Christ; nor was the visible scene
around us of a character likely to destroy in
us that sense of mystery and vastness which
alone is capable of perceiving the abysses of

time past. The sky was "softly dark and darkly pure" above us, the clear, dark sky of a summer twilight in Burgundy. On one hand were the old beechen groves, throwing their branches wide, on the other the sudden slope of the forest beneath us down into the deep valley; and a vast prospect led the eye over minor hills and plains till it met the crimson mist of the western horizon. Then the stars became brighter and brighter, and the flame of our fire glowed more ruddily, and the Antiquary, inspired by the influences of the scene and the hour, talked to us of the past with the unconscious eloquence of a speaker who is absorbed in a great subject, and sure of the full sympathy of his audience. When he came to the Middle Ages, he sang to us old ballads and pointed out whatever they revealed of the life and habits of that time, making many a delicate observation, such as can only occur to the loving and earnest student. The Antiquary excelled himself that night, and so communicated to all of us the power of his own enthusiasm that we were in such a state of imaginative exaltation as I never before witnessed in a circle of private friends; and this condition of feeling was the more remarkable for its contrast with our ordinary habits, which were those of light-hearted gayety and simple enjoyment of the days as they passed by. A singular proof that our imaginative powers must have been in extraordinary strength and excitement was what took place in the cottage on our return. The Antiquary had heard me speak of Rossetti's poems, a copy of which I happened to have with me on the Mount, and he begged me to translate one of them on that occasion. Now in ordinary circumstances I could not extemporize a French translation of an English poem that would be worth hearing, but something told me that night that a power of this kind was temporarily in my possession, so I opened the book and began.

The effect, both on myself and everybody present, was most remarkable. I felt transported into the highest realm of poetry, and became for that one hour a French poet endowed with Rossetti's genius, which passed through me as electricity passes through a conductor. In this way I translated — if such spontaneous utterance is to be called translation at all — the *Blessed Damozel, Sister Helen,* and *Stratton Water*, and both I and every one

present were in a state of intense emotion the
whole time, — indeed, as for the audience, I
never saw an audience so moved by poetry in
my life; and the next day, when prosaic reason
returned to us, we were all very much astonished at the enchanted evening we had passed
together. When I look over these poems to-
day they seem to me utterly untranslatable,
and I cannot conceive through what medium
of equivalents the power of them reached my
hearers.[1] Yet it *did* reach them.

There seems to be a necessity that everything should be poetical on the Mount. Even
Pauchard, whose occupations of cook and
housekeeper in one had certainly rather the
merit of utility than the charms of romance,
accounted for the song of the nightingale by
one of the most exquisite popular legends that
I ever met with. To enjoy it quite perfectly
one ought to hear Pauchard tell the tale himself, for nobody could tell it better, and he has

---

[1] If the reader happens to know French well, and to possess Rossetti's poems, let him try to read any one of the three
above-mentioned aloud in French from the English text, and
he will soon understand the difficulty of it. All poems are
difficult to translate into another language, but in some
instances, and this is one of them, the difficulty seems to
amount to impossibility.

the advantage of very nearly, yet not quite absolutely, believing it. When first he told it to the Antiquary, some years ago, it was in perfect faith, but now he sees that the Antiquary only admires without believing, and a tinge of scepticism has, I fear, invaded Pauchard's intellect also. Pauchard is a man of little knowledge, but of delicate feeling, and when he tells this tale he gives it every help from well-chosen inflections of the voice, and you feel that although he has never consciously cultivated any art of poetry, the spirit of poetry is within him, poor, illiterate peasant as he is. But to appreciate this legend perfectly we ought to hear it on the Mount, under the old trees, on a summer's night when the nightingales are answering each other in Malvaux. " Those little birds," says Pauchard, " have not always sung like that in the night-time. Long ago they sang in the day, but one of them had been singing so hard all day long whilst his mate was sitting on her eggs, that when evening came he was very weary, and went to roost on the vine, where he fell asleep directly. Now it was a warm night of May, and the tendrils of the vine were growing very fast, and they twined round the little thin legs of the nightingale whilst he slept. His comrades came to awake him, and said, '*La vigne pousse —pousse—vite, vite, vite, vite, vite!*' but he was so tired that he could not be awakened. At last morning dawned and then the sleeper awoke, but only to find himself helplessly fettered by the tendrils of the vine which had grown so quickly that now they held him fast, and he could not get away with all the fluttering of his wings. Then his comrades saw him die, and they said to one another, ' We will sleep no more in the night so long as the vine is growing.' And ever since then they do nothing but sing all night to keep themselves awake, and this is the burden of their song : '*La vigne pousse — pousse — vite, vite, vite, vite, vite, vite, vite!*' "[1]

Now is not that a perfect little flower of the popular imagination? I never met with anything more exquisite. It is full of the most tender feeling for nature, and the lightest, most graceful imagination. It might have been invented by some cultivated Oriental

[1] When Pauchard told the little tale, he pronounced *pousse —pousse — pousse* very slowly and seriously, as if gravely announcing a fact that was full of peril, but when he came to *vite, vite, vite,* he pitched his voice much higher and gave it an energetic *presto.*

poet, it might have been a fancy of Hafiz himself, suggested to his delicate sympathy by the
song of a nightingale in the warm Persian
night, when the vines were growing fast. Yet
it was not Hafiz who invented it, but some
nameless peasant of the Morvan, in an obscure
village, nobody knows how or when.

Much has been already said concerning the
things of interest on the Mount, yet one or
two of them remain unnoticed. The old
Gaulish roads are still so hard that trees cannot take root in them, but where not traversed
by the oxen that come for wood these roads
are covered with short grass like a lawn, and
the trees on each side meet overhead, making
long, very long, avenues of green shade where
it is pleasant to walk in solitude. In the deep
gorge of Malvaux (Mala Vallis) the Gauls
made a cutting for their road through the
solid rock where there is only just room
for the brook that flows from the Beuvray.
This is one of the most interesting traces of
their labors about the Mount, and as fresh as
if done yesterday, the tool marks still visible
in the hard rock. They had also evidently
fashioned a projecting pinnacle of porphyry
on one of the great buttresses of the Mount,

the stone that is called " **La** pierre de la Wivre," which is believed to have been a place of sacrifice, and there is a very curious and impressive legend about this stone.

The peasants believe that the Wivern dwells near it in a hidden cavern guarding his treasure, but that once a year the cavern opens and the Wivern goes out, leaving the treasure unguarded. As to the time of year when this happens the narrators differ. Some say that it is at midnight on Christmas Eve, others fix it on Easter Day during high mass ; in either case it is during mass, as there is a midnight service at Christmas. The popular legend in its present form goes on to recount how a certain woman, accompanied by her child, went to the stone of the Wivern instead of going to mass, intending to take his treasure. She found the cave open, entered and took as much gold as she could carry, and came out just in time to escape the Wivern on his return. On looking round for her child she could not find him anywhere. The cavern being now closed again, she knew not what to do, and went in despair to the priest, who told her to go to the place every day, and pour milk and honey on the stone till the expiration of the twelve months, and then when the day came for the opening of the cave, to take her treasure back to it undiminished and she should find her child. So she went day by day without fail, in heat and cold, in fine weather and foul, and poured milk and honey on the stone. At last the day came when the Wivern left the cave and the mother found her child inside, sitting quite unhurt, and in perfect health, with an apple before him on a stone table. So she restored the treasure gladly and took away her child.

The Antiquary, of course, looks at these stories from his own point of view, and he argues about them in his own way. All the Catholic character of this legend is, he says, nothing but an aftergrowth. In his view the legend is one of some Gaulish sacrilege and reparatory oblation. Some offering of treasure must have been sacrilegiously removed, when the Gaulish priests required a daily oblation (perhaps of milk and honey) until its restitution. The story is still closely connected with a stone that was most probably sacred, and has been rudely shaped into its present form by primitive human labor. But

the Antiquary confesses himself much embar-
rassed with the apple, which, he thinks, must
have some significance, if only it were dis-
coverable.

I may add that it is not very clearly decided
whether the milk and honey fed the child
himself, or the Wivern to prevent him from
destroying the child.

CHAPTER VIII

Our Pedestrianism — A Hamlet near the Mount —
Author taken for a Prussian Spy — Art gener-
ally supposed to be an Absurd Business — Beauty
of the Old Hamlet — La Roche Millay — The
Château and Garden there — A Night Adventure
— Another Return from the Mount — Wander-
ings in Search of an Old Pair of Fire-dogs — The
Château du Jeu — Its Garden and Avenue —
Château of a Small Squire — Manner of Life of
the Small Squires in Former Times — We sup and
sleep in an Uninhabited House — The Pied-à-terre
— Beneficial Activity — Wild Boars and other
Animals on the Beuvray.

I HAVE said something already about the
Antiquary's pedestrian powers, which have
been wonderfully improved and cultivated by
his summer residence on the Mount. The
summit is so small that it is like a little island
high in the air, and you cannot get out of the
island without hard walking down hill, which
of course involves a corresponding ascent,
from one side or the other, on your return.
Many Parisians who live at the tops of

houses cultivate pedestrianism on staircases, and the Antiquary is similarly situated, with the difference that every excursion into the outer world involves for him a descent of seventeen hundred feet. Just at first it seemed rather hard to go through these daily exercises of pedestrianism in obedience to the Antiquary's various projects for the amusement of his guests, but our limbs soon got into the habit of climbing, and then we began to see the matter from the Antiquary's point of view, or in other words to think nothing of the climb, but only of simple distance, as if the roads to Bibracte had all been perfectly level. I had a resource for all solitary excursions in my good beast *Cocotte*, who climbed like a mule, but without his obstinacy, so I often left the Antiquary with his diggers, and set forth with Cocotte and a complete sketching apparatus to explore the country in any direction that I pleased. So many different old Gaulish roads lead to the summit, — there are seven of them, — that our position was very central with these radiating from us in every direction; indeed this is one of the peculiar charms and privileges of the *Grand Hôtel des Gaules*, as we facetiously designate

the Antiquary's elevated residence. There
are two or three hamlets about the base of
the Mount which have remained unaltered for
the last three or four hundred years, and one
of them, Montmoret, is quite astonishingly
picturesque — so picturesque that one can
hardly believe it to be real. It has everything
to help it in the surrounding hill scenery and
the magnificent old chestnuts, and nothing
whatever to spoil the artistic impression that
it produces. There is one steep, tortuous
street with the richest variety of rustic construction, — enormous shadow-giving projections of thatched roofs under which great
teams of oxen may shelter themselves from
the sun at noon, curious external staircases
and galleries, picturesque wells, and all so
perfectly harmonious in color, with rich,
warm yellows and grays that glowed in the
afternoon sunshine, and only wanted green to
relieve them, which was given abundantly by
the chestnuts and the vines. The Antiquary
pointed out to me in one of these buildings
exactly the Gaulish principle of construction
in military walls of defence as we have seen
it described by Cæsar, the strong oak posts
and beams with regular intervals of stone-

work. I made some studies at Montmoret, returning to the summit of the Beuvray every evening in time for a late dinner; but the Antiquary had kindly accompanied me on the first of these occasions, thinking it probable, although this was in 1874, that the peasants when they saw me at work would take me for a Prussian spy. Without the shelter of the Antiquary's well-known and much-respected name it would be difficult to work unmolested in these hamlets near the Mount, for although the peasantry are both good-natured and polite, they are placed in a difficult position when they see an artist at work from nature, and this leads them to wrong conclusions. The motives of an artist's labor are utterly inconceivable by them, and cannot be made intelligible to them, so they are compelled by the defective condition of their knowledge to infer that you are making a map, for this they partly understand. The next question is why you are making a map, and for whom. For the Prussians, most likely, and when they become persuaded of this, the position of a solitary artist is not quite safe or pleasant. It requires all the tact and address that one may be master of to

keep things tolerably smooth, and allay these
suspicions enough to permit a quiet continu-
ance of work.   I had succeeded in doing this
for some hours at Montmoret when I threw
down a little tube that I had been using, on
which was the following inscription : —

ROBERSON AND Co's
MOISTWATER-COLOR
CHINESE WHITE
— 99 —
LONG ACRE, LONDON.

It instantly occurred to me that I had committed a great imprudence, but it was too late
to be remedied.   A young peasant near me
seized the tube, tried to read the inscription,
perceived that it was in a foreign language,
and then said to his comrades, " Ceci n'est
point Français, c'est du *Prussien !* "   Every
foreign language is " Prussian " for the French
peasantry.   However, I answered with the
greatest mildness of manner, " You are mis-
taken, my friend, these colors are not Prussian, they are English ; we buy them of the
English because the English make them better than anybody else ; the Prussians cannot
make them nearly so well, and we should be

silly, indeed, to get Prussian colors when they
are not so good, although they are cheaper.
These English colors are very dear." Then
I let them look at all my colors, among which,
by good luck, there was no Prussian blue, for
the learned young man who could read would
have recognized that word immediately. And
the question of price interested them very
much, as I find that the prices of things always
do interest poor people, who spend nothing
themselves except on the plainest food and
clothing; so Mr. Roberson's prices, which
seemed enormous to my hearers, happily got
their minds off that Prussian difficulty, and
allowed me to blot on in comparative peace
and quietness. But it is not quite safe even
yet to sketch about a French hamlet, although
you may pass for a Frenchman, as I always
do, and know the *patois*. It is still almost
essential to be accompanied, at least on your
first visit, by some notable of the neighborhood. An artist is, however, in some degree
protected against violent animosity by the
ridicule which his occupation generally draws
down upon him. After a good deal of experience in different countries, I have been forced
to the conclusion that art must be an absurd

business, for everybody seems to regard it with
ridicule mingled with pity.   Every artist who
works out of doors has anecdotes of his own
in illustration of this.   A peasant who had
watched Daubigny at work, left him with the
observation, "Il n'y a pas de sot métier," the
meaning of which is, " Although a trade may
be foolish, and futile in itself, a man is not a
fool for pursuing it if he earns bread thereby."
Another spectator encouraged me with laughing patronage, " Faites donc ! faites donc !
Vous ne faites de mal à personne ! " which
signified in explicit language, " Your occupation is ridiculous, but pray go on with it, for
it is perfectly harmless."   Sometimes, however, we are surprised by observations from
superior though uncultivated minds.   A man
at Montmoret, with a gentle and intelligent
face, said to the others, " This is a thing that
we are unable to understand, because we know
so little ; but if we had been well educated,
then we should have seen and understood a
great deal more about this work than is possible for us now."   There was the precisely
accurate truth about the matter, and we may
be sure that a peasant who could say *that* was
a very superior man by nature, for the noble

acknowledgment that we cannot judge unless we know, with the equally noble and rare acknowledgment that we do *not* know, are the two first conditions for a beginning of profitable culture.[1] On hearing this it occurred to me that it was foolish and wrong in me to be vexed with the ignorance of these poor people, instead of making some effort to remove it, though such an effort might seem well-nigh hopeless; however, I resolved to make the attempt, and deliver a lecture on the fine arts to an audience such as Mr. Slade certainly never contemplated when he established his useful professorships. I began by claiming, with some authority, to be heard, and told my audience that if they would only listen they should be made to understand something that they had never understood before. They listened attentively enough, quite a little crowd

---

[1] I once met with a market-gardener on a small scale who had never seen art work done, and I went with another artist to sketch in his garden, from which things of great interest were to be seen. I never was more astonished than by the amazing facility with which he entered into artistic ideas. He watched us at work, asked all sorts of intelligent questions, and after four such sittings had got more art knowledge out of us than most people who are educated contrive to gather in a lifetime.

of them, so whilst sketching steadily all the time, I gave them a lecture on the difference between making a map and making a study, and when I had done, there were at least half a dozen of the most intelligent who had clearly understood me, and these six explained the matter over again very clearly to the duller ones. There is a vast difference in rapidity of apprehension between these peasants and the English agricultural laborer. The Morvan peasant is almost inconceivably ignorant, but he is extremely quick and bright. Some of my hearers were facetious about the honor done to their little hamlet in being thus set down on paper. "This great capital city," said one of them, "has never been so honored since it was built." I asked how many inhabitants there were. Nobody knew exactly, but one clever-looking young fellow said it was easy enough to count, and went through the place, house by house, from memory, naming every individual inhabitant, and adding them by families as he went along till he arrived finally at the total, which was one hundred and eighteen. In a hamlet like this every one knows everybody else, and there is a familiar fellowship which is charming, or would be so

if they were not almost invariably accompanied
by neighborly hatreds and jealousies. Life
runs in this little quiet corner as it has done for
a thousand years, but ten years hence modern-
ism will have invaded it. I found one little
building with staring, new red tiles, and that
is the beginning of the end. La Roche Millay, on the other side of the Mount, must have
been well worth sketching in the Middle Ages,
for a strong castle with many towers occupied
the summit of a rock perfectly inaccessible on
three sides. This castle was replaced under
the Regency by a large mansion of that time,
a very good specimen of the Renaissance
château, with the great, bare, comfortless, lofty
rooms that the experienced traveller in France
always expects in edifices of that style and
time. I have just said they were comfortless,
but they have one comfort in the hot Burgundy summer, — they are delightfully cool.
The wife of the present owner never came
near it, not even to visit the place *en touriste ;*
however, she at last allowed herself to be persuaded, and when once she had visited La
Roche it became her favorite residence till
her death, which occurred very shortly afterwards. It is a most romantic and peculiar

place. The old castle was occupied by a
tremendously powerful feudal *seigneur*, and it
is quite the nest for a falcon of that breed, as
he would easily impose tolls on passengers in
the narrow glen. Just on the other side rose
the Castle of Touleur, on a rocky height now
densely wooded, and the Beuvray stands behind in considerable majesty — the Beuvray
on whose high and narrow table-land these
mighty barons were wont to meet for their
tournament of May. Only one tower remains
of the old castle of La Roche, but as regret
for its destruction was useless, I set myself to
enjoy the quaint garden, which was beautifully kept, but unaltered from its first design,
a formal design contemporary with the present
mansion. Huge walls, covered with flowers,
sustain the high terraces, and you have garden below garden, each in numberless parallel
beds, with curved outlines answering in their
general arrangement to the curve of the great
walls.

I confess to an old-fashioned liking for formality in gardens. I like a wilderness to be
as wild as possible, and a garden to be as
formal and regular as art can make it, with
no possibility of slovenliness. This was the

mediæval theory, and the Renaissance theory also, with other forms; it has been reserved for recent experimentalists to aim at a natural variety and wildness, which can never be satisfactory to any one who has access to nature itself. At a place like La Roche Millay, where nature is grand and wild in rock and mountain, and stream and tree, it is astonishing how pleasantly the formal garden attracts us by its discipline and rule, by its beds in determined shapes, and its flowers in brilliant regiments, for in the heart of nature we like to be reminded of humanity and of orderly pleasure and state.

We cannot always linger upon the Mount, so a day has to be fixed for our departure; but when we have started on our way home, there is no telling when we shall get there, for the Antiquary and I are travellers of a most uncertain and unreliable description. Once a friend of ours asked us to go and see a very beautiful property of his and dine with him, after which he was to accompany us to Autun. We went, accordingly, to see the place and accept his hospitality, and left rather late for a drive of more than twenty miles home. Now it happened that the Antiquary was

bringing away the piece of old tapestry from
the Mount, so he lay down on this tapestry
in the stern of my vehicle. I have already
remarked that on the Mount we have bad
habits in the way of sleep, that we go to bed
very late and get up very early, so that there
is a strong tendency to get compensation
afterwards. This was now the Antiquary's
position. Having slept insufficiently for
many days he could not resist the attraction
of the soft tapestry, but immediately lost in
dreams all consciousness of his present situation. I was coachman, of course, and our
friend and host was to sit at my left hand and
guide me. Now, the peculiarity of our position was this, the Antiquary knew the road,
but was fast asleep; our friend knew the road,
but he had drunk just one bottle too much
whilst exercising the duties of hospitality. I
was sober and awake, but utterly ignorant of
the road, and the night was so dark that we
could see nothing beyond the limited range
of the lanterns. My companion got into a
most interesting conversation about artistic
subjects, which he has studied and understands, so when we came to puzzling places
where several roads met or forked off in dif-

ferent directions, it plagued him to be interrupted, and he told me to go right or left very
much by chance, whilst he described the practice of a great artist whom he had known in
other days. I felt that there was some uncer-
tainty in his indications, but he was there to
guide me, and the responsibility rested with
him. After some hours of rather rapid trot-
ting, finding that we approached no nearer to
any place that was known to me, I resolved
to pull up and consult the Antiquary, so I
shook him out of his blissful dreams upon the
tapestry, and said that, having no longer any
confidence in our late host, I begged for better advice. The Antiquary got up and first
examined the width of the road to see what
class of road we were on, then he looked up
at the stars, a few of which were visible, finally
he ascertained that we were near a wood.
But this was all he could make out, so in spite
of two furious dogs he courageously went to
a farm-house and awoke the people, who gave
him information. It appeared that we had
been driving in a great circle (which the nau-
tical reader need not confound with the art of
Great Circle sailing), and were now within
three miles of the place from which we had

set forth. The consequence of this was that we wandered the whole night and only got home about five o'clock in the morning, to incur the most satirical observations from our respective households. If the reader suspects that the Antiquary and I had obscured our brains with Burgundy he will do us a grievous injustice, but a legend to that effect got credit in those parts.

On another of our returns from the Mount we were led into adventures of another kind. The Antiquary has always some curiosity in view, and this time it was a pair of fire-dogs which existed in a château somewhere between the setting sun and the rising moon, if we could only find it. Neither of us had ever been there, neither of us had anything but vague indications. We knew that the said château was in another department and in another province, but we hoped to come upon it ultimately, and so set forth on the quest. When the Antiquary is once in motion, with an old bit of brass or iron for the object of his travels, he will go on quite indefinitely; so I knew there was little chance of our arrival at any comfortable lodging for that night, and regretted not to have a tent with me in the

carriage, a precaution I sometimes take in
uncertain travels in the Morvan. It rather
amused me to surrender myself quite absolutely to the Antiquary's guidance, and see
what would be the end of the adventure. The
first thing he did was to request me to leave
the good high-road under pretext of making
a remarkably short cut which was to land us
several miles nearer to our supposed destina-
tion. I never like to hear of short cuts when
I am driving, especially when the vehicle has
four wheels and is inclined to be top-heavy.
Short cuts are nice for pedestrians, and not
disagreeable when you are on horseback, but
it is pleasanter to drive on good macadam
than over granite boulders and through
ditches and marshy places. The Antiquary
first made me go down into a hollow which
was flooded with water, that made the road
exactly like a pond, and when we got out of
that a hillock rose before us covered with
blocks of granite the size of an arm-chair with
scarcely a perceptible passage. A mile farther
a gigantic chestnut, which had been felled,
blocked up the road entirely, so the Antiquary
led Cocotte into a cornfield under pretext of
turning the obstacle, but finally found himself

unable either to advance or to recede, so we had
to take the animal out of the carriage and back
out of it, after which we went through another
field.   All along this road the scenery was
quite delightful, there were remarkable numbers of fine chestnuts, with rocks and hills
and a lake.   Farther on we came to a château
near a clump of Alpine firs on rocky ground,
and this house, whose name dates from the
Romans (*Chateau du Jeu*, Jovis) has the
most magnificent hedge I ever beheld.   This
hedge is all of hornbeam, about twenty feet
high and perhaps a thousand yards long, in all,
a great massive wall of verdure with arcades
cut in it, and so regular a surface that it looks
as if it had been built, and as if you could
walk on its broad and level top.   Here again
my taste for formality in gardens was fully
gratified.   It seems to me that a wall of verdure like that, with its arcades and regularly
dressed surface carries out the architecture of
the mansion in a manner which wild nature
never can do, and I greatly enjoyed and
approved at the *Château du Jeu* this transition
from the perfect wildness of the pine grove
with its rocks, that looked exactly like an
Alpine foreground, to the ordered symmetry

of architecture in stone. Gardening of this
kind is a true response to architecture, and
exactly the intermediary that is needed between the lordly mansion and the wilderness.
I may just add that Turner thoroughly appreciated the peculiar artistic value of such artificial gardening as this. See how absolutely
artificial is the garden with the great *jet-d'eau*
in the vignette before the Pleasures of Memory! There is an arcade of hornbeam there
too, but not so lofty nor so long as the real
one that I have just described.

Other considerations were suggested by this
peculiarly beautiful place. It is approached
by an avenue of chestnuts, perhaps a mile
long, and very well grown, though not yet old
enough for the trees to have attained their
perfect majesty. Now this avenue both gained
and lost much by a certain peculiarity. It was
not straight, as French avenues usually are,
but as serpentine as the winding of a river.
Here again I decidedly prefer the more formal arrangement, the straight line, whilst fully
admitting the charm of a slow and slight curve
in an avenue *after* a straight line. There is an
effect of this kind in the magnificent abbatial
Church of Vezelay, where the ground plan of

the stone avenue of columns is curved to one side with a result in perspective that the reader will immediately understand. Such a curve explains better than any other device the distance between the columns or the trees, and in a sylvan avenue it is delightful to see the increasing spaces in the curve which follow a regular order of increase, no two spaces equal, yet all subject to one law. On the other hand, when the curves are too frequent and too rapid you have no *vista*, which is a lamentable defect of the avenue at the beautiful *Château du Jeu.* On entering it I had no notion that it was important enough to be worth notice, but expected that it would come to an end after the first curve. Then came a number of other short curves, always with the same expectation, and it was only after much driving that I perceived how noble an avenue it was. Nor did the mansion gain anything in stateliness from this approach. It was like marching up to a fortress in the zigzags of trenches, without seeing anything till you come close under the walls.

It was quite dark when we came at length to the mansion of the fire-dogs' which were the object of the Antiquary's quest. It was

guarded and inhabited by one lonely old
woman, though there were men in the adjacent
farm-buildings to prevent her from dying of
fear, and this old woman was in bed on our
untimely arrival; but nothing can deter an
Antiquary, so he cruelly awoke her by making
a burglarious noise at the window and pro-
nouncing the name of the absent *Châtelaine*
with an air of irresistible authority. The poor
old thing dressed in great haste, and admitted
us into a lofty but narrow chamber with the
mingled furniture of a kitchen, a sitting-room,
and a bedroom, all of it old and quaint like
the inhabitant. I began to wonder whether
the scene before me was a real scene, or
whether this were not some odd volume of a
romance that I was reading. The Antiquary
did all the business of the interview, so I was
quite free to look on as a simple spectator, and
this left me a prey to a very strong feeling of
illusion. The whole adventure was perfectly
in the spirit of Scott, and might have been
transplanted just as it was into the Chronicles
of the Canongate without any sense of the
incongruous. Every visible thing except ourselves was at least a hundred years old, not
a great age certainly in comparison with the

Gaulish antiquities of the Mount, but enough
to give a great air of quaintness to everyday
household gear.   The old woman led us into
four very vast and lofty chambers, in one of
which was the pair of fire-dogs that had
brought us to the place.   They were of brass,
and represented the towers and curtain-walls
of a fortress, with cannon all in position, the
work being Louis Quinze, elaborate enough,
but not particularly elegant.   In countries
where wood is burnt the fire-dogs are often
very splendid and highly wrought with fanciful ornament and invention, but I have seen
much better examples than these brazen
towers with the little cannons firing away from
the battlements like toy guns.   When we
came away, I looked at the house from the
outside, and came to the conclusion that there
was only just room in it for the great chambers that we had seen.   The Antiquary confirmed this opinion, and when I asked how the
family in former times could manage with so
few rooms, he told me that in the class of small
squires life in a country house was arranged
down to the end of the last century very much
as it is still in the houses of the peasantry.
There were four large beds in each room, one

in each corner, forming with its four posts and its curtains a sort of independent tent, whilst the space in the middle of the room was left vacant for daily habitation. Guests of both sexes occupied beds in the master's own chamber. This led us into a conversation about the changes of manners and customs within the last seventy or eighty years, and we agreed that although modern dwellings were apparently less spacious, they were infinitely more convenient and much better adapted to the requirements of civilized existence than the châteaux of the old French squires. They had no idea of the comfort of independence in a room, and with their system of living privacy was utterly unattainable and unknown, as it is still in the houses of the peasantry. They had not separate bedrooms, a dressing-room was undreamt of, and the idea that it was desirable to get into one room without passing through another does not seem to have presented itself to their imagination. How ladies and gentlemen ever managed to get a thorough washing where there was no such thing as privacy, seems inexplicable. The Antiquary's explanation is that they omitted the ceremony altogether, which

appears to be the plain and simple truth.
Surely the great practical purpose of a house
is to give facilities for civilized human life, for
cleanliness, for decency, for study, and not
one of these is attainable without privacy.
Every good modern house has these, and
therefore in practical service to civilization it
is superior to such minor châteaux as the one
we visited that night.

But where were we to sleep? The Antiquary had a private theory of his own on this
subject, and I submitted to him as commander of the expedition. We drove many
miles in the dark, along roads entirely unknown to me, and stopped at last before a
house near the road-side, when the Antiquary
lifted his voice. A man looked out of the
upper window with a candle, and shortly reappeared on our own level. A whiter man I
never remember to have seen. His cotton
night-cap was white, his hair was white, his
beard was white, his shirt, trowsers, stockings,
were white, and so was the candle in his hand.
Everything about him was white except his
slippers, which were of a pale yellow. He
looked very nice and clean, and was most
hospitable, pressing us earnestly to stay all

night in his house and offering us a supper. The Antiquary declined with the greatest firmness, and then the white man handed him a key, and said, " Well, you 'd much better have stayed here ; however, I wish you a good-night." On we went for another mile, and then by the Antiquary's orders I turned up a narrow lane, happily not long, and we arrived in a great straggling farm-yard with a quaint pigeon-cote tower and a rough-looking sort of mansion on one side, with two very ugly and awkward staircases all covered with grass and tall weeds. The house looked as if it had never been opened for a hundred years, and there was not the slightest sign of human habitation.

First the Antiquary put Cocotte into one corner of a big stable, and then he led me up one of the stone staircases, and opened an old oak door studded with big-headed iron nails. We entered a big desolate room with beds in alcoves, and appearances as if the last inhabitants had quitted it in some precipitation. After this room was a suite of three others, and in the last of these was another bed and a very large couch or settee covered with faded tapestry of the time of Louis XIII.

Not a living soul was visible about the place.
When we came to the last chamber the Antiquary said, "This will be your room," and
left me there with a candle. Soon afterwards
he reappeared with a strong, gaunt woman
from the next farm, and she very soon lighted
two great fires. There was a strange, musty
smell in the rooms, as if no window had been
opened for a century; so we opened every
window, heaped logs on the blazing fires, and
changed the air as thoroughly as we could.
The woman spread a clean table-cloth on the
table in my room, put clean sheets on the
beds, and the Antiquary soon produced all
necessary table utensils and two bottles of
excellent wine. Supper was served at midnight, and we had eaten nothing whatever
since breakfast on the Mount, having been
travelling the whole time; so we did justice to
the simple repast before us, though with regret, perhaps, for the culinary abilities of Pauchard, whom we had left in his lofty dwelling.

The explanation of this mysterious uninhabited house in which the Antiquary con-
ducted himself so independently was simply
that it belonged to him, with a particularly
beautiful little estate of five hundred acres,

and that he kept a little furniture in these
rooms and a few bottles of wine for chance
occasions like the present. A Frenchman
likes what he calls a *pied-à-terre*, that is to say,
two or three rooms of his own where he can
establish himself in a temporary home, and be
independent of everybody; nor does he consider it essential to his happiness that the
rooms should be luxurious, or that servants
should be kept in them during his absence.
A town *pied-à-terre* is usually a single floor in
a large house that is divided into flats and
guarded by a porter; a country *pied-à-terre* is
usually a small house close to farm buildings
and guarded by the farmer. People who live
in towns have a country *pied-à-terre*, and
country folks have one in the town. The
Antiquary's principal residence is in the town,
but he has three country residences, where he
can be as comfortable as he cares to be for
weeks at a time, and even receive guests hos-
pitably. The glorious Mount is one of them,
this farm is another, and the third is in the
vine lands on a vineyard estate of his. As
each of these is within a day's drive of the
town house, the Antiquary can easily visit
them whenever he likes. The system is not

exceedingly expensive, and a man always feels
infinitely more at home in rooms of his own
than he possibly can do at an inn. The feeling of being *chez soi* has a great charm.   It
is this which constitutes the delight of yachts
and tents, — to have variety of surroundings
and still be under your own roof, even when
that roof is only of wood or canvas.   There is
sometimes a good deal of *friction* in these
arrangements, unless they are superintended
by some one who has had experience in the
organization of independent ways of living,
and who can both look to details and set
things right with his own hands. Now I
venture to affirm that the Antiquary and I
are both of us more than commonly compe-
tent in the art of making a rough temporary
residence habitable, for we have both had a
good deal of practice, without which people
always bungle sadly in these matters, and we
have also a natural liking for the sort of
activity which they call for. The reader who
has never found himself compelled to make
arrangements for his own comfort will
scarcely conceive what a beneficial influence
such labors have both on mind and body.
They entirely relieve the mind from intellect-

ual strain and from the habit of reflection
which pursues the student like his own
shadow, whilst they give it solidity and ballast
by compelling its strict attention to material
necessities and things. " If I could but work
with my hands," said an accomplished scholar,
" it would be such a blessing to me!" Now
what he instinctively felt to be desirable, the
Antiquary and I value from happy experience.
We find that the activities of a rougher and
more self-dependent life are good for us after
the ease of home. We find that any fatigues
and privations we have to incur are just sufficient to keep us in good humor by the
effort of the mind to react against them.
The Antiquary is certain that the preservation of his health and strength has been in a
great measure due to his work on the Mount,
which has supplied the great desideratum for
beneficial exercise, a purpose outside of itself.
If I have a criticism to make upon his present arrangements, it is that they are becoming rather too convenient and too comfortable,
and that his little mountain establishment
displays each year some improvement which
removes it faster from the character of a
camp; but I trust it is safe from the invasion

of easy-chairs and carpets, whilst French
polish will be long unknown there, and unless
by chance some specimen of it be discover-
able upon a gun-stock or a pistol-case. The
tapestry on the walls is perhaps an allowable
piece of luxury, for it has a certain wild
grandeur in harmony with the sylvan surroundings of the place. The subject being a
forest scene, with quaint mediæval figures, it is
possible to imagine that this forest of patient
needlework may have represented some sweet
glade of the Mount itself, when knight and
baron chased over it with hawk and hound.
Even in our own time there is many a lair of
wolf and wild boar within a league of the
Antiquary's huts. Sometimes there is a great
hunt, and on the last of these occasions more
than twenty wild boars were killed. There
are deer too, and foxes, for many wild animals
breed within or without the ancient walls of
Bibracte, no longer fearing the throng of
armies or the noise of battle after twenty
centuries of silence.

A U T U N.

AUTUN.

I.

IF the reader will take a map of France, he
will see that the Saône and the Rhone
make a line in the east side of the country
which goes almost due south to Marseilles,
whilst the Loire, on the contrary, begins by
flowing from south to north, and then shows
a strong westward tendency, sometimes going westward suddenly, and then resuming
its northern direction, but at last making
a magnificent curve in the region about
Orleans, and after this curve going very
decidedly to the Atlantic. The southern-
flowing rivers, Saône and Rhone, which form
a single watercourse, and the young northern-
flowing Loire, are for a time very near neigh-
bors, the distance from one to the other, as
a bird flies, being less than thirty miles in
the department of the Loire. After that the

distance widens as you travel northwards, but
still the two watercourses keep neighborly;
and they both run across the department of
Saône et Loire, in which the Loire flows
about seventy miles and the Saône eighty.

The country that lies between these rivers
is interesting in many ways. It includes the
whole department of the Rhone, part of the
department of the Loire, and three-quarters
of Saône et Loire, a region in which the scenery is varied, and the marks of human history
sufficiently numerous to answer a traveller's
expectations. The physical geography has
very decided features. There are the two
great rivers, important even at that distance
from the sea, and hills which are almost
mountains, rising to about 3,300 feet above
the sea-level, and about 2,800 feet above the
water of the Rhone. The forms of these
hills are sometimes fine, sometimes monotonous, but they always have the advantage of
giving good distances, especially in that state
of the atmosphere, very common in France,
when there is a certain amount of mist in
the air, hardly perceptible in itself, yet just
sufficient to give a sense of wide space and
remoteness.

A pedestrian travelling over the highest land in this region, and keeping between the two rivers, and as nearly as possible at an equal distance from both of them, would ultimately reach a lofty table-land which ends very abruptly to the north, not exactly in precipices, but in very steep slopes densely wooded. Just before the table-land comes to this sudden termination, it bears upon its ample surface a magnificent park, rich in fine old timber, with lakes surrounded by what seems a natural forest, and an old château, not a castle, but a spacious old man sion enclosing three sides of a quadrangle, and containing a great number of rooms hung with old tapestry, a decoration more abundant in this château of Montjeu than in any other house of equal size that I ever visited. The house is at the head of a deep ravine, crossed by a wall of great height and strength, and above the wall the ravine is filled up so as to present broad flat areas of garden ground, laid out in the old French style, from which there is a view over a vast expanse of hilly country, the view being enclosed by masses of trees on each side of it, as a theatrical scene is by its *coulisses.* But this is not

the view in which we are likely to be chiefly
interested.

. Suppose that our pedestrian leaves the
château behind him, and crosses the park
to the northern gate (which is more than
two miles from the house), he still finds
himself, so long as he is in the park, on
ground which is either perfectly level or very
gently undulated. When, however, he issues
from the park by the north gate, he has before him a very different scene. The land
suddenly falls in a slope so steep that the road
down it is a zigzag like those in the Alps;
and far below, as you look over the tops of
the trees, you see a hill rising with a city
upon it, and beyond the city a plain bounded
by distant hills and watered by a gleaming
river that washes the lowest portion of the
walls.

It is the city of Augustus, Augustodunum,
now abbreviated to Autun. Like its name,
the city itself has been reduced into a much
smaller compass; but as the name still retains etymological vestiges of its origin, so
the place itself bears traces of the Roman
times. There is, however, this difference between the name and the place, that whereas

the name is only shortened and does not
contain a single letter that was not in the
Roman name, the place is not only brought
within a small area, but altered in its nature
by the successive ages which have passed
over it. The Middle Ages, the Renaissance,
and modern times have all devastated what
went before, as a schoolboy sponges his slate,
except that the schoolboy sometimes sponges
his slate *entirely*, whereas it does fortunately
so happen that successive ages rarely sponge
out the work of their predecessors in a quite
perfect and absolute manner.

As seen from the height of Montjeu,
Autun, like many cathedral towns, appears
so dominated by its cathedral that it is difficult to imagine how it must have looked in
the Roman times when no such edifice existed. It seldom happens that a church is so
happily placed as that of Autun, nearly on
the exact summit of the hill on which the
city is built, and finishing it with a noble
ornament. Spires are not always the most
successful of architectural constructions ; and
there are many situations in which a massive
tower, square up to its sky-line, has a better expression of dignity and strength, and

holds its own better, — at least it seems so to
me. But the spire of Autun, besides being
extremely elegant in itself, is precisely the
architectural feature that was most required
in that situation, and is a conspicuous instance of the positive *improvement* of natural
scenery by human toil and taste. I shall
have more to say of it, and of the cathedral
generally, before I have done with Autun ;
but it was necessary to mention it in this
place, as the object which first strikes the eye
of a stranger from whatever quarter he first
catches sight of the city. Next to the cathedral, the most striking object is the lofty
octagonal tower of the Ursuline convent,
which was erected on a Roman tower, the
Roman work still being perfectly visible up
to the first string-course. This tower has
in recent times been rather increased in apparent height, by the construction of a small
dome upon its summit, which serves as a
pedestal for a statue of the Virgin.

A city at a distance shows itself principally
as a collection of towers with a confused med-
ley of roofs and chimneys between them ; and
it is probable that the Gothic cities of mediæval France were more effective at a distance

than any towns of Roman or Greek antiquity,
simply because towers of various kinds were
of such great importance in Gothic architecture and generally so well designed. In the
Middle Ages Autun had many of them ; and
a few remain to the present day, in spite of
the excessively destructive tendency of modern
French municipalities, bodies which really
seem to find a keen satisfaction in clearing
away the vestiges of past ages. A few towers
still remain in the southern mediæval wall of
Autun ; and the massive square one which
bears the name of St. Leger forms part of the
Bishop's palace, where it is probably safe for
some time to come. The towers visible from
a distance are all mediæval ; the Roman ones
are still numerous, but hidden by the trees of
a long avenue, which have prospered so as to
completely overshadow the Roman fortifications on the west side of the city. The
Roman towers are now mere semicircular
projections from the wall, and I do not know
to what height they may have risen above
the walls when both were originally constructed. The Roman city was of far greater
extent than the mediæval one afterwards built
within the limits of it, like a garden made in

one corner of a field; but although Augustodunum was of importance as to size, and
although it included public buildings of considerable splendor and extent, it is probable
that it never presented so picturesque an
appearance as the Autun of the Middle Ages.
In the first place, it is now positively ascertained (as the result of notes taken during
many years by observant antiquaries whenever the soil has been disturbed for building
purposes) that the Roman city was built on
the modern American plan of straight streets
intersecting each other at right angles, the
only difference being that in America the
houses are probably higher and the streets
wider. A map of Roman Autun looks something like a chess-board with irregular sides.
In the mediæval city, on the contrary, the
streets went in every direction; and the few
old pieces of them that remain give some
faint idea of the incessant variety which must
have greeted at every turn the contemporaries
of the Crusaders.

Augustodunum had its gates, temples, and
places of public amusement, of which not
much remains to the present day. There
are two gates; one near the river, now called

the *Porte d'Arroux*, the other, on the northeast side of the city, called the *Porte St.
André,* because one of the towers which
flanked it, after being used as a temple by
the Romans, was turned into a Christian
chapel and dedicated to St. Andrew. How
many other gates there may have been in
the Roman times we do not exactly know.
There were perhaps eight, possibly five or
six; but this is a question simply of antiquarian interest at the present day, as all
trace of the others has disappeared. The
greatest loss is probably the *Porte des Marbres*, which appears to have been an architectural work of importance adorned with
sculpture in marble. Much carved work has
been found where this gate existed, and used
as ordinary building material. The *Porte des
Marbres* looked to the east, and is believed to
have been the principal entrance to the city.

There was a great amphitheatre, of which
only the site is visible at the present day. In
the early part of the seventeenth century the
ruins were still imposing, and sufficient to
suggest an easy imaginative reconstruction
of the whole. A century later there were
still ranges of stone seats and arcades, though

in fragments; and now, in our own century,
there is literally not one stone left upon
another.   It was one of the finest of the provincial amphitheatres, considerably excelling
Nîmes.   It had three tiers of arches, and I
see in an engraving made in the beginning
of this century that caryatides were intro-
duced between the arches of the uppermost
story; but whether this was in consequence
of a tradition that had come down to the
draughtsman from the seventeenth century,
or a mere fanciful invention of his own, may
still be doubtful.

Very near to the amphitheatre was a theatre
constructed on the usual Roman plan, but on
a much larger scale than was common in
Gaul.   In consequence of measurements and
calculations made by M. Chenavard, an architect of Lyons, it appears that the Autun
theatre must have afforded room for nearly
thirty-four thousand spectators, while those
of Orange and Arles could only seat about
half that number.   This gives some idea of
the population of Augustodunum.   The present municipality is erecting a new theatre,
not on the same site; but the comedies of
Alexandre Dumas and Émile Augier will not

be performed before such imposing audiences as those which listened to the plays of Plautus and Terence in the classic times of the city. There is, however, the consolation that the horrors of the amphitheatre are not likely to be repeated, unless some future century should go back to the barbarous pastimes of the Romans.

Near to the theatre and the amphitheatre, but independently of both, the Romans had a fine artificial lake at Augustodunum for naval combats. Nature so favored the establishment of this lake by an abundantly flowing rivulet from the hills, and also by the natural hollowing of the ground near the theatre, that the Romans easily made a reservoir of great importance, and it has been calculated that the sports upon it could be witnessed by a hundred thousand spectators.

Antiquarian writers give very fine accounts of the temples at Augustodunum, but artists who only care for what they see, will not find much to interest them in the way of temples. The structure which is called the " Temple of Janus " is like a very massive square tower, perfectly plain, with holes in it for windows. It does not in the least resemble our ordinary

conception of a Roman temple as a structure
of some elegance, adorned with columns and
a pediment; and although the presence of
any relic of antiquity, however ugly, has
always some influence upon the mind, there
are few ruins in the world so large as the
Temple of Janus which have so little artistic
interest. It has been classed amongst historic
monuments, as it deserves to be, but it is
merely a piece of substantial building, not of
architecture in any high sense. The little
circular temples of Pluto and Proserpine,
which still existed by the river-side two hundred and fifty years ago, and of which some
fragments remained much later, had probably
greater pretensions to beauty. The only other
temple of which there is any remaining fragment is that of Apollo, which now consists
simply of a lofty piece of wall with a niche in
it, surrounded by modern houses and completely hidden by them. Neither is it by any
means absolutely certain that the temples bore
in Roman times the names of the divinities
which have since been attached to them.
The one attributed to Pluto was called so on
the strength of its resemblance to the Temple
of Pluto at Rome ; that of Apollo, because it is

not very far from the middle of the Roman town, and Eumenes, in one of his orations, placed the Temple of Apollo in a central position. A marble head with abundant hair, and half a colossal hand, had been found near the temple which is attributed to Apollo before Edme Thomas wrote in the beginning of the seventeenth century. As for the little round temple close by the Arroux which was attributed to Proserpine, it has also been supposed to belong to the god of the river Arroux, and Edme Thomas held a decided opinion that it must have been dedicated to Augustus. These are merely conjectural opinions of antiquaries on subjects of which nothing is positively known ; but as it is impossible either to talk or write about any edifice without having a name for it, and as it is tiresome to have to say each time we use it that the name is merely conjectural, these titles have obtained currency.

It would be in the highest degree interesting to visit such a place as Augustodunum, which must have been a very perfect specimen of a Gallo-Roman city, with the special advantage of a very exceptionally fine situation ; but the mediæval city must have been incom-

parably more to our taste, and perhaps even
the town, as it exists at present, may have
certain advantages over its predecessors, in
spite of the constant destruction which has
been going on for the last three hundred years.
It has more variety, which is something, and it
bears the traces of a longer past. We ought
to remember, what we very easily forget, that
when mediæval architecture was new it had
nothing whatever of that romantic power over
the mind which it now derives from its antiquity and from the contrast between the
pathos of its ruinous beauty and the unfeeling
prose of a century so prosaic and so mechanical as ours. For us the walls and towers of a
mediæval town are connected with the descrip-
tions of our modern poets and novelists, who
have thrown over them all the enchantments
of genius, and they are contrasted by us with
the ugly and dirty buildings we see in our
" hives of industry," which the mediæval mind
could no more imagine than it could foresee
the electric telegraph. But I shall have more
to say on this subject when we study what
remains at Autun more in detail.

II.

THE CATHEDRAL.

THE classical conception of an architectural structure was that it should be complete in itself and perfectly harmonious, so that nothing could be added to it without visible excess, and nothing taken away from it without evident loss. The classical building was an organic whole, approaching in its completeness to the completeness of animal forms, and the idea that such an organic whole could be improved by the addition of a foreign adjunct was an idea which could not occur to the classical mind. The well known and often quoted opening lines of the "Ars Poetica" of Horace express the classical horror of the incongruous. He was writing about poetry and painting ; had he written of architecture it would have been in the same strain, but nobody in the Augustan age could possibly have foreseen the wild experiments in architecture which have been made in mediæval and modern times.

The love of unity and perfection did not die out at once. The simple Romanesque churches were as consistent as Greek temples, and, in the best examples, not less complete in plan. Subsequent modes of building have also produced works admirable for their unity, but the misfortune has been that the desire for unity in the Gothic ages was weaker than the desire to work in the prevailing fashion of the day. Gothic architects seem to have believed that current fashions were always a positive improvement on the art of their predecessors. They appear to have been, at the same time, entirely unaware of the great artistic truth that superior things out of place are less desirable than inferior things which are where they ought to be. The human head on the horse's body of Horace was not a more monstrous violation of organic harmony than those which the Gothic builders committed whenever a Romanesque edifice fell into their ruthless hands. The mixture of delicate appreciation of artistic beauty, when it was of the kind that happened to be in fashion, with perfect indifference to that which had gone out of fashion, displayed or betrayed in the works of mediæval architects, is one of the strongest evidences we have to prove the wonderful power of fashion over the tastes and

feelings of mankind. The mediæval architects
were as much the slaves of fashion as Parisian
fine ladies of the present day, the only difference in their favor being that their fashion
changed more slowly, a slowness due to the
long time required for realizing changes of intention in architecture in comparison with the
rapidity with which they may be carried out in
costume. But if the mediæval architects were
less rapidly changeful than our modern dress-
makers, they were artistically inferior to them
in the care for unity and harmony. Every
modiste in Paris takes the trouble to think, as
she devises a costume, how the parts of it will
go together. She will not sew the sleeve of
a splendid dress to a plain one; she will not
encumber a dress conceived originally in one
style with ornaments derived from a different
and a totally incongruous style. Yet this is
what, in a far more serious art, where the
responsibilities are far greater and fanciful
divergence much less excusable, the mediæval
architects did without hesitation and without
regret. They appear to have acted blindly,
to have had artistic impulses, but no power of
criticism, and especially to have been carried
forward by the impetus of a great general move-

ment in one direction or another, an impetus
which they do not seem to have had any disposition to resist.

These remarks may seem strangely severe
to the reader who has been accustomed to hear
the Middle Ages spoken of with great reverence
as a time when builders were not only much
more intelligent as artists, but much more
conscientious and conservative than they are
to-day. As for the intelligence of the mediæval architects there can be no doubt that it
was surprisingly high, considering the world
they lived in ; but it was an intelligence
strictly confined to their own style, like the
practical intelligence of the uneducated in our
own day, who do their own work well but
appreciate nothing beyond it. With regard
to their conservatism it was exactly that of a
French revolutionist who knocks down an old
political system in order to erect a new one in
its place. It was not simply destructive, nor
purely constructive either, but a combination
of both, beginning with demolishing other
men's performances in order to make room for
one's own, as the monks scraped parchment
manuscripts to cover them with their own
elucubrations.

The history of Autun Cathedral, from the beginning down to the present year, is a good example of the fact that the architects of our own time, notwithstanding the hard things that have been so often said about their pre-sumption, are in reality the first who have paid any respect whatever to the conceptions and intentions of their predecessors. The Church of St. Lazarus, or Chapel as it was once called, was originally planned in the eleventh century, the idea being attributed to Robert I., Duke of Burgundy. It was so far finished in 1132 as to be consecrated by Pope Innocent II. in person, and in 1146 the re-mains of St. Lazarus were transferred to it. Who this St. Lazarus really was I do not pre-tend to say. It appears to be certain that he was a bishop of Marseilles, and the priests encourage the belief (without absolutely affirm-ing it to be well founded) that this bishop of Marseilles and Lazarus of Bethany were the same person.[1] To any one who believes in

---

[1] The tone adopted by the Church on this subject may be judged of by the following quotation from an ecclesiastical history: "C'est à cet ensemble de circonstances que l'on attribue l'arrivée en Bourgogne du corps vénéré de l'évêque de Marseille, Saint Lazare, regardé par la plus imposante des

this identity the remains of the bishop must be of great interest, and they are carried through the city annually in September in stately episcopal procession, to be venerated by the faithful.

I mention these relics of Lazarus in this place because the church which is now the Cathedral of Autun was built specially to receive them, most likely in the full belief that they had belonged to Lazarus the resuscitated, as it is not likely that the Duke of Burgundy would have rendered such extraordinary honors to any mere bishop of Marseilles. A tomb of great magnificence was erected to receive the bones on the spot now occupied by the high altar. This tomb was an edifice of white, red, and black marble, more than twenty feet high, and elaborately carved by a monk of artistic genius named Martin. The tomb of Lazarus was the glory of the church, and its *raison d'être* as the church was built to contain and protect it; but, unfortunately, it was intrusted to the keeping of the clergy in days when there was

traditions comme le même Lazare dont il est parlé dans l'évangile et que Jésus-Christ ressuscita quel ques jours avant sa Passion."

no State authority to protect ecclesiastical buildings against them. Of all human beings, an ignorant clergy are the most dangerous guardians of churches. As a French architect observed to me, " It is like asking wolves to guard sheep." The consequence of their guardianship in this case has been that the tomb of Lazarus has vanished, some of the marble in it being employed for purposes which will be explained later.

As the church of St. Lazarus at first existed it was a complete conception, having the merit of perfect artistic unity. We shall soon see how ruthlessly this unity was afterwards destroyed, in deference to newer fashions of building. If I were to describe the first architecture as simply Romanesque, the word would convey but a partially true impression. What is usually understood by Romanesque architecture is a style retaining the round arch from ancient Roman work, but with very little else of a classical character. There are, however, examples in which the classic influence is much more generally visible; and of these Autun is one of the most remarkable. It is generally believed — and is, indeed, so probable as to be allowably

assumed for a certainty — that the reason
for this must have been the remains of antiquity at Autun itself; which, in the eleventh
century, were far more abundant and far
more perfect than at the present day. When
the church of St. Lazarus was built, the amphitheatre was in existence and probably in
fine preservation. The architectural remains
of the theatre may still have been imposing,
the Roman gates still comparatively numerous, the temples not yet demolished. Surrounded by these examples of classical Roman
architecture — some of which were certainly
very conspicuous by their size, and others
attractive by their elegance — the church-
builders of the eleventh and twelfth centuries
would naturally be subjected to the kind of influence which art-work already accomplished
has over fresh production, especially when
the fresh production is a new beginning. In
this sense it is not too much to say that
Autun Cathedral is the fruit of an eleventh-
century Renaissance; a Renaissance preceding Gothic, as a subsequent classical move-
ment followed Gothic and replaced it. If
we examine one of the bays of Autun Cathedral, we find that the massive piers are

decorated with fluted pilasters; and so are the
little piers or wall-spaces between the small
arches in the upper story of the Roman
Porte d'Arroux. The arcade of the triforium
consists of round arches on thin fluted classical pilasters. The cornices and mouldings
are classic in taste; and the widest divergence
from classical precedent is in the great arches,
which are pointed, showing the beginning of
the Gothic tendency. A fluted pilaster is
carried above the triforium on each side to
the springing of the roof; where it supports
a simple flat rib or projection forming a distinct round arch over the nave, the space
between these arches being simply vaulted.
The windows of the clear-story are plain,
round-arched, Romanesque windows, in harmony with the arcade of the triforium (except
for the absence of classical decoration). In
the space left between the heads of the
pointed arches and the string-course on which
stand the pilasters of the triforium, there is a
band of sculptured decoration, composed entirely of large roses and running quite round
the edifice, being interrupted only by the
large pilasters.

The original Romanesque church had a

triple apse, consisting of a large semicircle
for the nave, and two smaller semicircles for
the aisles. The apse has been altered or
hidden since it was built, as I will explain
later; for the present I am trying to describe
the church in its first perfect state. Viollet
le Duc believed that the round central apse
went up to the full height of the nave, and
he drew it so in a design which was engraved
and published in the *Revue Générale de
l'Architecture* for 1853; but this was a mistake which he afterwards acknowledged with
the readiness of a true student, which he
always was. The cause of his error was the
band of roses which goes round the apse, and
therefore seems to imply that the primitive
architecture was continued at that height
with the triforium above it, and windows
above the triforium, as Viollet le Duc represented it in his drawing of a restored interior;
but, in fact, the roses in the apse are of plaster, and much more recent than the stone
originals elsewhere. There is evidence that
the original apse was not very high, that it
was lighted by two rows of small Romanesque
windows, and separated from the choir by
a large arch springing from capitols still

existing. The apse, in fact, must have been one of those Romanesque apses common in churches of that period, which do not aim at an appearance of imposing height, but rather, if I may so express it, at an appearance of intimacy and snugness, as if the altar ought to have a home of its own, distinct from the body of the church, and comfortably proportioned, as to height, to the limited area enclosed by the semicircular wall. There are charming examples of this at Semur-en-Brionnais and in the church of St. Genou in the department of the Indre.

The whole of the church of St. Lazarus was originally finished in the kind of Romanesque which I have just described. To complete the description I have only to add that there were no side-chapels beyond the aisles, and that the aisles were lighted by windows with round arched heads (and, of course, no mullions or tracery) of the same kind as those in the clear-story, but larger. There was a fine arched doorway at the end opposite the altar, which from the position in which the church is built happens to be the north, and not the west end; and another of similar character, but less magnificent, in the east

transept.   There was a tower above the in-
tersection of the transepts and nave, but of
this tower no drawing has come down to the
present day.   All that is known about it is
that the tower must have been of great weight,
for a reason which the reader will meet with
shortly.   It was, probably, a heavy stone
structure of two or more stories, the weight
of the wall not much lightened by the aper-
tures: and there are reasons for believing
that the pointed pyramidal roof must have
been covered thickly with lead.   In the
twelfth century (so I am told by a learned
French architect) the art of laminating lead
was unknown in France, and it had to be
beaten out with hammers, so that it was
always thick in comparison with the sheet-
lead of modern times.

The present cathedral is celebrated for its
vast and magnificent porch, which, being of
Romanesque architecture and a striking thing
in itself, is naturally (and I believe invariably)
supposed by visitors to have formed part of
the original structure.   The truth is, however,
that the first building had no porch whatever,
and that the noble flight of stairs in the
present porch, which produces so grand an

effect that the first builders of the cathedral
got the credit for it, is in fact altogether
modern. It is not even a restoration. There
never were any such steps there at all until
the nineteenth century; in the old time there
was nothing but a slope of irregular ground
with access to the doorway through a hole
in the eastern wall of the porch, altogether a
much less imposing arrangement. Externally,
the Romanesque church must have appeared
simple, but harmonious. The walls of the
aisles were quite plain and relieved only by
the slightly projecting buttresses of the style,
answering in situation to the piers of the
interior. The windows were so plain as to
have scarcely any decorative effect except the
slight one derived from the recurrence of their
uniform arches. The most decorative things
in the whole building were the arcades between the windows and roof of the nave, and
those on the front of the transepts. There
was also considerable richness in the door-
ways, to which the plain walls gave additional
interest. In the great arch over the northern
door was a most elaborate tympanum representing the Last Judgment, and in the arch
over the east door was another tympanum, of

less importance, representing Adam and Eve in the Garden, when they hid themselves after eating the forbidden fruit and God found them.

If the church of St. Lazarus had come down to us in its first state, it would not have had the variety and historic interest that it possesses to-day, but it would have been a very complete and congruous work of art. Certain changes occurred, however, which made it impossible to keep the building as it was at first. The soil was treacherous. The north wall with the great doorway in it showed unmistakable signs of falling outwards; the great vault of the nave began to push out the walls of the clear-story. The exact measures of these displacements are for the north wall between 1 ft. and 1 ft. 4 in., and for the outward pushing of the vault of the nave, about the same *on each side*, making a total widening of about twenty-eight inches. Ruin was avoided by two plans, which in reality amounted to the same expedient. The north front was prevented from falling outwards by the addition of a gigantic porch, for which the architect had the excellent excuse that in those days there were great numbers

of leprous pilgrims who came crowding about
the door and needed some shelter from the
inclemencies of the weather. I do not know
if these poor lepers were admitted into the
body of the church, but through the open
doors they would see, in the distance, the
great marble tomb of St. Lazarus, — the
Lazarus of Bethany, as they believed, who
had lost health and life, and recovered both
by a miracle like that they vainly hoped for.
Thus the weakness of the building, or rather
the insecurity of its foundations, led to an
addition which, so far from having the appearance of an excrescence, looks like a first
thought of artistic genius. The supporting
of the side walls, to prevent them from falling
outwards, cannot be considered so fortunate.
Here the architect had recourse to the more
commonplace device of flying buttresses, —
not, however, so commonplace in those days
as it has since become, for these are amongst
the earliest examples. The architect at Autun who strengthened the cathedral in this
way at the close of the twelfth century accomplished his purpose effectually by strong walls
set at right angles to those of the aisles and
projecting far, these walls being weighted

above by massive pinnacles, from the bases of which sprang the arches that supported the walls of the clear-story.

Another evil effect of the state of the foundations, or of the soil in which they were laid, was that the weight of the great tower pushed down the four piers on which it was erected, so as to disjoin them from the inner walls in the four angles, causing a break of six inches. Notwithstanding this, it might have been left with that degree of disruption for centuries if a great fire had not occurred by which the tower was destroyed. Material evidence of this fire has been found during recent restorations. It is supposed that the woodwork of the roof must have been set on fire by lightning. The lead ran down upon the adjoining roofs of transepts and nave, which were also fired. I do not know the exact date of this event, and the date is not of any consequence as concerning the architecture of the building. What concerns us is the date of the new tower and the new roofs, which we know. Cardinal Rolin, in 1480, built the new tower and many other things, of which more will be said presently. Like all builders of the Gothic times, he and

his architects paid no respect whatever to the
character of the building they had to deal
with. It seemed to them perfectly natural
and right to erect a Gothic tower with a tall
spire on a Romanesque cathedral. Their
tower was beautiful in itself, and their spire
of extraordinary lightness and elegance. The
state of the foundations suggested the necessity of avoiding useless weight, so the spire,
which in itself was to be one hundred and fifty-
eight feet high from the top of the tower, had
to depend for its strength on excellence of
construction rather than on quantity of material. It is entirely of stone, and without any
internal support whatever. Seen from the
inside it presents the appearance of a room
of which the walls converge as you look up,
and I was never in any building that con-
veyed the impression of prodigious height so
powerfully. From base to apex there is nothing but the smooth stone walls, and, although
the actual height is not much more than the
nave of Amiens cathedral, the narrowness of
the area and the convergence of the sides
make it seem incomparably more lofty. The
effect on the mind is increased when we are
told that the walls are seven inches thick at

the base and six towards the summit. "If people could see the stone used in the spire of Autun," said an architect, "in a solid mass, they would be surprised by the small quantity of it."

The Cardinal's way of dealing with the apse was as follows : His Gothic taste prob-ably disliked a Romanesque apse, as not imposing enough and not sufficiently well lighted, especially if the six small round-headed windows were filled with colored glass, so he did not pull the apse to pieces, nor even remove the stonework of the win-dows ; he simply built them up, as people used to do in old houses when the window duty was first established. He removed the stone roof of the apse, which had been built in the Romanesque fashion, *en queue de four*, took down the great arch called the "*arche triomphale*," and left the walls of the apse standing as they were, and even the capitals from which the arch had sprung. He then carried up the wall to the full height of the nave, piercing it with five great lancet lights and two smaller ones, their sills being on the top of the old apse wall. As the old apse had only been supported by the slightly projecting buttresses usual in Romanesque architecture, it was thought necessary to fortify them by strong ones, to support the wall, above which (on the Gothic principle) was a weak structure cut by seven slits in the shape of windows.

From that date the Gothic devastation went on very vigorously in the aisles. The improvers pulled down the old walls with the simple windows, decorated the openings with fringes of senseless cusps, and erected a series of chapels in the flamboyant style, to occupy the spaces between the great buttresses. Most of these chapels are heavy and inelegant, which cannot be said of the Gothic apse. A very strange piece of Gothic construction is that which supports the organ loft. It consists of half arches with abundant cusps, some of which come in awkwardly and contradictorily, yet this work is said to be of the same period as the spire. The flamboyant chapels were begun at that time also, but continued later, in the sixteenth century.

A vestry was erected as a distinct building outside the cathedral to the west, and it may have helped to strengthen the wall of the

western transept. This vestry is a not inelegant specimen of flamboyant Gothic. The
general scheme of it is simple, but the parts
are disposed with that freedom from the
idea of regular and symmetrical arrangement
which marked the Gothic, as opposed to the
classical spirit. Although there is one window
in each defined space between string-courses
above and below and buttresses on each side,
the window is not inserted in the middle of
the space, but freely to any side that might
suit internal convenience. The little tower
is pretty, but it owes much of its prettiness to
its uppermost story and its pyramidal roof,
which were added quite recently by the restorers. The same restorers have done a good
deal to the vestry in other ways, giving it a new
roof and a new pierced parapet, the parapet
being an exact copy of the original one, which
had fallen into decay. If this vestry were an
independent building it would probably have
some celebrity as an elegant specimen of
French Gothic applicable to domestic architecture, for a modern house might be built
as a development of the same idea, but in its
present situation it is overwhelmed by the
mass of the cathedral, with which it has very

little architectural relationship, and is also
hidden from public view by being in a small
enclosure where it can hardly be seen in its
entirety.

It was very unlikely that this cathedral
would get through the seventeenth and eighteenth centuries without grievous injury by
destruction or addition of some kind. The
clergy in the later Renaissance had a passion for classical marble columns and panels,
just as in the Gothic times they had a passion
for high roofs and tall windows. They have
always indulged themselves in these passing
fancies whenever they have been able, with
the most absolute disregard to artistic unity.
I have said that Cardinal Rolin walled up all
the windows in the Romanesque apse. It was
reserved for the clergy of the eighteenth century to line this apse nearly up to the sills of
the new Gothic windows with huge panels of
magnificent red Sicilian marble, divided by
columns of gray antique marble, with gilded
capitals, and surrounded by frames and mouldings of another variety. On a cornice supported by these columns stand a number of
little, fat, gilded angels, like Cupids, which
hold garlands, and are otherwise elegantly

occupied. The marble for this panelling was, I have been told, partly got from ancient Roman remains and partly from the grand tomb of St. Lazarus, which was used as a quarry.

It is curious that Voltaire should have had some influence over the cathedral at Autun, but it is believed that he caused some destruction there, and was also the involuntary cause of some preservation. He went to stay at the château of Montjeu, where he attended the marriage of the Duc de Richelieu. During his visit he condescended to look at the cathedral, and so ridiculed what appeared to him the barbarism of its architecture, and especially of its sculptural adornments, that the canons had the whole of the great tympanum plastered over to hide the composition of the Last Judgment. In doing this they preserved it from damage during the Revolution, and it remained so hidden for seventy years; after which lapse of time its existence was totally forgotten, and some gentlemen at Autun discovered it, suspecting that there might be carvings under the plaster. As to the other tympanum, that over the door of the east transept, representing Adam and Eve

hiding themselves in Paradise, it was broken
to pieces and carted off, the fragments being
afterwards used in building shops in the town.
One of these fragments, representing Eve
under a bush, was found during an alteration,
and has been preserved. In the mouldings
round the great tympanum there is a broad
hollow originally filled with a succession of
figure-groups, which the clergy of Voltaire's
time diligently cleared away in order to complete the classical simplification begun by the
plastering of the tympanum. They also had
doors made in the approved Renaissance style,
and altogether did what little their limited
means allowed them towards the taking away
of all character from the edifice committed to
their charge.

We now come to the nineteenth century,
the epoch of Viollet le Duc, the most learned
and the least prejudiced of all architects who
ever lived in France — at least so I sincerely
believe. Viollet le Duc, unlike all his predecessors, had so great a respect for unity in art
that he would avoid, whenever possible, the
addition of any feature to a building which
was not in harmony with the original design.
His fault, if it was a fault, consisted in a steady

desire to get back to the first state of the structure, before irreverential successors to the original architect had made additions which he could never have even conceived. In dealing with such a building as the cathedral of Autun, in which the additions in another style were too important to be removed, Viollet le Duc must have felt an irritating desire to go further than the general opinion was prepared for. If the cathedral of Autun had been his private property, I doubt whether he would have long resisted the temptation to pull down the Gothic tower and spire and replace them with a tower of purely Romanesque design; but I do not doubt, I am perfectly certain, that he would not have tolerated the Gothic apse. He would have restored the Romanesque apse, which still exists behind plaster and marble, in all its integrity; he would have cleared away the marble panels, columns, gilded Cupids, and the rest, and horrified the ecclesiastical mind by the destruction of the tall windows above them.

He and M. Durand were restrained from this line of action by a respect for public opinion, though I fancy that if they had pulled

down the Gothic apse suddenly and without
warning, the public would have accepted the
fait accompli after a little tempest of complaint
about the marbles. In all other respects the
action of the modern restorers has been in the
direction of the Romanesque restoration wherever possible. I have said that the first roofs
were burned when the lead trickled down
from the burning tower. Those roofs were
replaced by Gothic architects with new ones
of far higher pitch. Of late years it has been
found necessary, in consequence of the decay
of the Gothic roofs, to proceed to a new re-
placement, and this has been done with the
Romanesque pitch. The chancel retains its
Gothic roof, the nave and transept have the
new pitch, which is a restoration of the
Romanesque roof. This new pitch was objected to as taking away from the apparent
dignity and importance of the edifice; and
there is no doubt that high roofs look more
imposing than moderately inclined ones, but
there is a great compensation in the dis-
engagement of the tower. The tower would
look much better if the chancel roof were
brought down to the level adopted for that of
the nave. The two small Romanesque towers

are entirely new. There was no authority to
go upon, as the original towers had never
been completed. Under these circumstances
M. Durand designed two towers with pyramidal stone roofs entirely in pure Romanesque
taste, yet not free from one or two rather
serious objections. The first is that they are
seen from the country on all sides along with
the Gothic spire, with which they have nothing
in common, and which is, unluckily for them,
so very elegant that they appear heavy in
comparison. To this objection the architects
answered, that as the north front was Romanesque they could not do otherwise than finish
it with towers in the same style; but I am
not quite sure that this is the case. With all
the deference which is due to the superior
acquirements of professional men I imagine
that there would have been sound artistic
reasons for another course. As the great
spire was too beautiful to be destroyed, I
would boldly have conformed the smaller
towers to it, built their upper stories in Gothic,
just as if Cardinal Rolin's architect had dealt
with them, and finished them with elegant
Gothic spires — younger sisters of the great
one — inferior in stature, but not in grace.

Such a course would have given the cathedral a delightful harmony in all distant views, and would not have injured the north front when seen near, for the simple reason that, with the neighboring houses where they are, it is never possible to see the porch and the twin towers at the same time. The second objection to these towers is, that although Romanesque in style they are not in the flat classical Romanesque of the church itself, but in a less refined, more massive, and rounder Romanesque, approaching in character to our own Norman. It may also be objected that the similarity of the two stories is monotonous, and that one story with rather higher openings would have avoided this repetition. I imagine, too, that it is rather a fault in construction to put an arch very near to another opening and just under it. The eye expects an arch to carry something massive and weighty, like a good space of blank wall or else a roof. I know that this objection would apply to many superposed arcades, but I have always felt it to be of some importance so far as the satisfaction of the eye is concerned.[1]

---

[1] If the reader has ever watched the building of a common stone bridge, he must have felt how much more satisfactory

In the course of the restoration, it was
necessary to reconstruct the four piers under
the central tower, and to allow of this being
done, the tower and spire were carried upon
an oak scaffolding of enormous strength,
the arches being kept in their places by
gigantic iron screws. This was one of the
prettiest pieces of engineering in modern
architectural operations.

The unity of the cathedral might have
gained if the spire had fallen and been replaced
by a tower in the style of the twelfth century,
but the effect of the spire in the landscape
could with difficulty be rivalled. It is in itself
a great finial, not of the church only, but of
the whole city, which it finishes in what seems
so natural and inevitable a manner, that it is
difficult to realize how Roman Augustodunum
must have looked without it.

and substantial the bridge seemed when a few courses of
masonry had been added above the arch than it did when the
arch only had been just constructed. There is a substantial
reason for this, which is that an arch is stronger and more
likely to keep its shape when it has a good weight on it.

III.

THE LAPIDARY MUSEUM AND THE ROMAN GATES.

A MONGST the many hard things that are said so frequently against the nineteenth century, the accusation of a want of reverence for the past is one of the most common. Certainly it may be admitted that the authorities of our time (especially municipal authorities in old cities) have destroyed many vestiges to make room for well-lighted, modern streets, and anything that stands in the way of what seems a desirable straight line is likely to be removed; but it may be put to the credit of our age that we do not regard this destruction of memorials without some feeling of regretful interest, and some desire to preserve a trace of them for our descendants. In this we differ from the men of all preceding ages. If they preserved anything, it was by happy neglect; when they wanted a site, already occupied by a building, they simply removed the impediment to the present scheme without taking thought for the inquirers of the future. The idea of founding a museum was an idea so foreign to the minds of the Middle Ages that they could not have entertained it. The present fashion was everything with them. So far from having any tender sentimental interest in the past, like the romantic interest of our poets and novelists, or any picturesque interest like that felt by our painters, they had not even the scientific interest of the archæologist. The results of this deadly indifference are, for us, infinitely deplorable. The Middle Ages were exactly the time for founding archæological museums, because in those ages the destruction of classic monuments was steadily going forward ; and if there had only been museums and archæologists just then, the smaller and more precious parts of ancient work might have been preserved forever. Augustodunum was a Roman city of real magnificence ; this we know positively from what has come down to us, from the great mosaics, the large and elaborately sculptured marble capitals, and the important scale of the places of public amusement. During the centuries when Roman Gaul was becoming mediæval Burgundy and France, the Roman Augustodunum was destroyed gradually, being used as a great quarry in which hewn stones might be had for the taking.

That was the time for founding a lapidary museum, instead of which the museum was founded in 1861, when the Middle Age destroyers had done their best to efface every vestige of classic times, and when the people of the Renaissance and of modern France had in their turn destroyed the mediæval city. After these two great destructions — as nearly complete, both of them, as leisurely perseverance could make them — the modern archæologists in the latter half of the nineteenth century come and collect a few fragments, buy a little plot of land, and set their mutilated old stones round it under a shed!

All honor to them for their care and industry, but such archæology is a melancholy business. " Too late! too late!! " is the inscription that it finds on every fragment. It is like picking up pieces of blistered canvas when a picture-gallery has been destroyed by fire — sad reminders of a splendor utterly passed away, and which a little care and prudence at the right time might have preserved so easily!

The founders of this modest little Lapidary Museum were very happy in their choice of a locality. There was a certain chapel, dedicated to St. Nicholas, and built in the twelfth century, which for ages had been disused as a place of worship, and employed for various common uses as private property. Wonderful to relate, it had not greatly suffered from these changes; probably, even, it had suffered less than it would have done in the hands of Mediæval and Renaissance ecclesiastics. A farmer may fill a church with hay, a cooper may fill it with tubs and barrels, without altering the conception of the architect, but an ignorant priest can collect money for supposed improvements, and do more harm in a few months than mere neglect would achieve in as many centuries. It was determined, therefore, to purchase this chapel of St. Nicholas and a bit of land about it for the safe keeping of the old stones. The chapel was dealt with tenderly; to say that it was "restored" would convey a false impression. It was simply put into a condition of necessary repair, with a plain new roof and floor. It possesses a very interesting Romanesque apse, once decorated in fresco, above the colonnade, and there was also a border of fresco decoration about the great arch before it. No attempt has been made to brighten or complete these old

frescos, which remain exactly as when found
— faded, mysterious, and probably far more
interesting than in their crude freshness. The
apse itself is in a state of quite perfect preservation. It has the usual round arches and
slender columns, with pretty sculptured capitals. If the student looks for some reminis-
cence of classic architecture, such as we found
in the Cathedral, he will not be entirely disap-
pointed. To the right and the left, but hidden
from the nave by the projection of the larger
pillars, are two pilasters, fluted like those on
the piers of St. Lazarus, — just these two, as
if to remind us that we are in a Roman city.
Another point of similarity to the cathedral is
the great arch itself, which, instead of being
round, is pointed. The rest of the building
is not of especial interest in itself, except
the Romanesque doorway, still very well
preserved.

Its contents compensate for the bareness
of the walls. There are a few odd shafts of
columns, or fragments of shafts, of various
materials, syenite from Egypt, and different
marbles and granites either found by the
Romans in Gaul or brought by them from a
distance. These shafts are used as supports

for pieces of cornice or for capitals that did
not belong to them, and so the architectural
effect is, of course, very incongruous; but the
visitor soon understands that he is in a collection of odds and ends.   There are some
very fine Roman capitals so preserved in
the chapel, but unluckily all mutilated; still
enough remains to prove the past magnificence of the city, as it has never been custo-
mary to erect great marble columns with
elaborate carvings in a village.   In the apse
are preserved some fragments of that great
tomb of St. Lazarus which once adorned the
Cathedral, and it appears from these (there
are more of them in a heap somewhere up in
the attics of the Cathedral itself) that the
workers in marble of the twelfth century were
fully acquainted with the kind of engraving
on marble and filling up with black cement
which was practised by the Baron de Triqueti
in the works he did for Queen Victoria at
Windsor.   The drawings for the tomb of
St. Lazarus are not of much value as drawings, but the knowledge of the engraving
process shown by the artists is perfect, and the
inserted black substance is as sound and hard
everywhere as the marble.   There are also

statues of Martha and Mary from the Cathedral, of the twelfth century, showing little science but a good deal of human feeling. The most interesting thing here to antiquaries and theologians is the famous ἰχθύς inscription, which they come from all parts to see. The reader may find a full account of it in the forty-second session of the "Congrès Scientifique de France," volume I., page 49. As for me, I am far too wary to entangle myself in these deep matters even to the extent of modestly copying the letters, as I should immediately receive a number of epistles convicting me of ignorance. All I venture to say is that the stone is a white-looking piece of marble, broken into fragments, which are pieced together again, and on which may be made out a Greek acrostic, of which the lines begin with the letters ἰ, χ, θ, ύ, and something which is supposed to stand for a Sigma, making the mystic fish. It is believed to belong to the third or fourth century; and as it seems to favor the idea of transubstantiation, it has, of course, a peculiar interest for theologians.[1]

---

[1] Here is an accepted French translation, for which I am not responsible : —

"O race divine de ἰχθύς céleste, reçois avec un cœur plein

In the middle of the museum is a large
mosaic, found where the railway station now
stands, and presented to the museum by the
company. The design of it is regular, with
common Roman decorative forms, but without
any particular artistic merit or originality of
conception. It has been said that the colors
of this mosaic are dull, but the simple truth
is that the tesseræ want repolishing. A kind
of varnish is sometimes used to revive mosaics
for museums, when they are not trodden upon,
and it might wisely be employed in this
instance. There is little that is notable in
sculpture, most of the figures being rudely
carved images of Gallo-Roman household
divinities, but there are some exquisitely beautiful fragments of Renaissance work which at
one time decorated the chapel of Denis Poillot
in an old church near the present cathedral,

de respect la vie immortelle parmi les mortels. Rajeunis ton
âme, ô mon ami ! dans les eaux divines, par les flots éternels
de la sagesse qui donne la vraie richesse. Reçois l'aliment
délicieux du Sauveur des saints : Prends, mange et bois, tu
tiens ἰχθύς dans tes mains.

"'Ιχθύς accorde-moi cette grâce, je la désire ardemment,
maître et sauveur ; que ma mère repose en paix, je t'en con-
jure, lumière des morts. Aschandeus, mon père, toi que je
chéris, avec ma tendre mère et tous mes parents dans la paix
d' 'Ιχθύς souviens-toi de ton Pectorius."

now pulled down. The design of these is of the most masterly elegance and unsparing elaboration. So fine is the work that if it were in some close-grained wood it might serve for delicate furniture, whilst the designs are so complex that merely to copy them in drawing would require very long and painstaking labor; indeed, only the photograph could do them perfect justice. After the rude Romanesque work, and even the comparatively rude and stiff designs of the Gothic ages, it is like a new revelation of human skill and knowledge to come upon sculpture so accomplished as this, and to think that the lovely Renaissance chapel, of which these fragments were only a part, was carelessly sacrificed and the stones of it cast aside as worthless —stones rich with the unsparing toil of a master!

There is a fine antique sarcophagus in white marble, with many figures, representing the hunting of the boar of Calydon, but this was not found in Augustodunum. It came originally from Arles, and thence to Lyons, and by the gift of Bishop Devoncoux, of Evreux, it passed into the Lapidary Museum at Autun. There is another sarcophagus of

antique origin, with its original inscription
defaced and Gothic ornaments added. This
was used, according to tradition, for the remains of a saint of the seventh century called
St. Francovée in French accounts, who dwelt
in solitude in the Morvan. Since his bones
became dust the sarcophagus was the property
of a nobleman, Baron Pigenat, who desired to
be buried in it; but when he was dead his
friends discovered a difficulty which had never
been thought of, — they found that he was too
tall for his sarcophagus, and from an intelligible feeling they did not like to amputate his
legs, so they buried him in a common coffin
and left the sarcophagus for many years in the
churchyard at Tavernay, the village near his
residence. Afterwards his successor gave it
to the Lapidary Museum, which owes the
treasure entirely to the stature of the first
baron.

Round the little plot of ground, which is
now the garden of the Lapidary Museum,
there is a shed on pillars to shelter the remains, for which there is not room enough in
the chapel. Here are a number of Roman
tombstones of the third or fourth century after
Christ, generally very rude in their carving,

yet intelligibly representing the occupation
pursued by the dead man during his lifetime.
More interesting than these are the remains
of a sarcophagus in gray marble, which once
held the body of the great and powerful
Queen Brunehaut, one of the most energetic
women of the Middle Ages: accused by
Clotaire II. of the death of ten kings, and
condemned by him to be dragged to death by
horses; a subject which, dreadful as it is, has
more than once been effectively represented
in painting, when the horses have come to a
stop at last in some melancholy valley, with
the pale corpse of the dead queen lying mo-
tionless behind them.   Her sepulchre was at
Autun, at the Abbey of St. Martin, not far
from where the Lapidary Museum now stands,
so that the only memorial of her now remaining is very nearly in its right place.

There is little else of note in the museum
except some Roman capitals in white marble
and other materials, like those preserved in
the chapel.   One great use, however, of such
a museum has been admirably shown by the
housing of part of Jean Goujon's famous
Fountain of the Pelican.   This fountain was
erected near the Cathedral in Renaissance

times; but, although the date of it is comparatively recent, the stone was too tender and friable, and, to prevent it from falling, the upper part of it was removed and lodged in the museum. It is in an advanced stage of decay, many of the stones having retained little of their original form, but others are still sharp enough here and there for the design to be easily made out; and a very beautiful design it is. It is proposed to make a new copy, as accurate as possible, of the whole, and carry all that remains of the original to the Lapidary Museum, a much more reverent and rational mode of proceeding than any attempt at restoration of Jean Goujon's work. To my feeling it is one of the most perfect little structures of its kind to be met with anywhere; the proportions are so harmonious and the lines of the columns, cornices, and arches so ingeniously contrived to produce a great effect of variety. The pelican on the summit is piercing her breast for her young. In drawings of the fountain she is often represented as a natural sort of pelican, but in the original stonework she is strictly conventionalized, so as to go well with the architectural idea. Again, in the drawings I find the vases

made heavier than Jean Goujon made them;
and indeed it is never safe to trust to anything
but photographs for representations of anything really elegant in architecture, as the
elegance of it depends upon nicely observed
proportions, which few draughtsmen are careful to notice.

Of the remaining Roman gates, that which
is commonly called *la Porte d'Arroux* (as
being near the river) is the more beautiful.
It is the gate leading to Paris, and stands on
the steep slope of land going down to the
bridge. Its flat pilasters, fluted and crowned
with carved capitals, are extremely elegant,
and very probably taught a lesson in delicacy
to the architects of the Romanesque cathedral.
There is also a very rich cornice, elaborately
carved, between the large archways and the
little arcade above them. Generally what
strikes the visitor in this gate is the fine preservation of the masonry, the sharpness of the
stones, showing that if it had been left un-
touched from the time of the Romans it would
still have been in good condition. Within
the arches there are large grooves for the
doors, which were evidently raised and low-
ered by winches and chains. In the other

gateway the *Porte St. André*, leading to
Besançon, this system does not appear to have
been followed. From certain holes in the
walls, on each side, it is evident that the door
was barred by strong beams placed across it.
These were first inserted into holes on the
right, and then the other ends of them were
dropped into grooves on the left, which are
still visible. These Roman gates were originally flanked by towers for their defence, and
the height of the *chemin de ronde*, or passage
for troops above the archways, gives the exact
height of the Roman wall, which appears to
have been thirteen metres to the top of the
battlements. It is deeply to be regretted that
the *Porte des marbres*, which was far more
splendid than the two now remaining, being
richly adorned with sculpture, should have
been destroyed during the Middle Ages; but
in those times there was no law in France
for the preservation of historical monuments.

IV.

HOUSES.

THE Roman city no doubt greatly surpassed the mediæval in the magnificence of its public buildings, except that the temples, however rich in marble capitals and mosaic pavements, could never produce so fine a distant effect as the towers of the churches; but, notwithstanding the luxury of wealthy Gallo-Romans and the perfection of their habitations according to their own ideas of orderly and comfortable arrangement, I am fully convinced that the mediæval city must have been incomparably more interesting than its predecessor if considered as a collection of dwelling-places. The tiresome regularity of the Roman streets is in itself quite enough to prove that the houses must have been comparatively uninteresting. A learned antiquary, M. Roidot-Déléage, seized upon every opportunity for studying the foundations of Augustodunum which presented itself during a space of forty years, and the result of his labors was a map in which every block of Roman houses is marked in its exact locality, and every

Roman street is drawn from one wall of the city to its opposite.[1] So completely had M. Roidot-Déléage mastered his problem that he became able to predict the exact spots in which the corner-stones of Roman street-blocks would be found when excavations took place, and his predictions were always verified. All the local antiquaries accept his map as being perfectly trustworthy, and if it is so the inference is that the Roman habitations were arranged with the most mechanical regularity in square blocks or "islets" of building, as the French call them, all exactly alike in their general ground-plan, and measuring about a hundred English yards on each side, the ordinary streets being about ten metres wide and the two principal ones about sixteen, half of which was occupied by causeways. The length of the principal street, which crossed the city from north to south, from the Paris gate to the gate leading to Rome, was 1,570 metres, and, like all the others, it was per-

---

[1] This map, which is one of the most thorough pieces of archæological work ever executed, received a medal from the Société Française de Numismatique et d'Archéologie in the year 1868 as the best existing map of a Gallo-Roman city. It was published in the "Mémoires de la Société Éduenne," New Series. Vol. I. 1872.

fectly straight. Here we have just the plan
of some new American town, the best of all
plans for convenience of access to every house,
and also for ventilation, but the worst for
architectural and picturesque effect. It is
believed that the houses, except a few residences of great personages, were always low
and small. The straight lines of the streets
are in themselves evidence that the straight
line must have predominated in the fronts.
Streets without curves, houses without projections, and probably with low roofs and a
poor skyline, like modern English or American building of the most utilitarian character;
these, as far as our knowledge goes, appear to
have been the most prevalent characteristics
of Augustodunum.

Mediæval Autun was a very different place.
Its streets curved in every direction, and the
same street varied in its width. So far from
keeping to any rigorous alignement, the houses
sometimes projected in advance of the line and
sometimes withdrew, as it were, into recesses.
There is evidence that the mediæval streets
widened and narrowed like running streams,
and that sometimes a house projected into
the street as a rock does in water, an incon-

venience that the mediæval people do not
seem to have minded.   The idea of the street
as the Romans had it, and as we moderns
have it again, does not seem to have occurred
to the mediæval people at all; they do not
appear to have cared for the street in itself,
but only for the houses, and the street was
nothing but a means of communication from
one house to another.   Neither was there any
sort of conformity in the house-building; there
were no Improvement Acts, there was no
Baron Haussmann to decree that the windows
should be all alike on the same story for a
hundred houses, as in the Rue de Rivoli.
Every man built his dwelling according to
the conditions determined by his taste and
his means, often adorning it with varied and
fanciful ornament, and always showing art in
it of some kind, were it only in the mouldings
of a beam or the careful finish of wood or
stone work about a window.   The remnants
of the mediæval city are not nearly as numerous at the present day as they were a hundred
years ago, but there are still enough of them
to give a good idea of what it must have
been, — a quaint place with many comfortable
houses and a few splendid ones.

A sketcher has many opportunities which do not occur to others. People are interested in what he does, and their interest soon passes into kindness. I have almost invariably found that if I sketched an old house I could examine every nook and corner of it, generally by the spontaneous invitation of the inhabitant. In this way a sketcher who cares for more than the outside appearance of his subject may learn many curious details about the internal arrangements of old dwellings, and consequently about the domestic life of the past. One characteristic seems to have been invariable. A small modern house is a place with a number of tiny rooms in it, but a small mediæval house had always at least one relatively very large room, and even the great mediæval houses had comparatively few rooms, but those were of handsome size. The reason is that the mediæval people cared much less for privacy than we do, and lived more together, after the manner of our own lower classes. In such a house as that in the Rue Cocand, at Autun, now inhabited by M. Guenard, the locksmith, the large room on the ground floor, which is now his workshop, was formerly the general family living-room, and

the large room above it the general bed-
chamber. It would have a bed in each corner,
made into a sort of tent with great curtains,
for the degree of privacy which satisfied the
mediæval mind. A few little places for kitchen
and servants completed the necessary arrangements. Even in the smaller country châteaux
the four-bed system prevailed.

Our modern preference for separation in
sleeping apartments, even at the cost of making them very small, is certainly a great advance in civilization, but it is not an unmixed
advantage. The cramped and confined French
townsman of limited means hardly ever knows
what it is to be in a large room, but his mediæval forefathers enjoyed that luxury every day.
A French gentleman of my acquaintance, who
is a great archæologist and has studied past
ages till his tastes and feelings have grown
into sympathy with those of his remote forefathers, built for himself a shooting-lodge
entirely according to his own fancy. " The
house itself will not be large," he said, " but I
am determined to have one large room in it."
That was quite a mediæval idea, and the way
he carried it out was this: He built his one
room lofty and vast, with a stone chimney-

piece huge enough to carry life-size Gothic
statues for ornaments, and round this room
he built little cells for sleeping, in deference
to modern notions. In practical use the great
room was a continual satisfaction to him. In
wet weather the party could meet in it without a sense of confinement, in hot weather it.
was comparatively cool and airy. This luxury
of space the mediæval people enjoyed in one
room at least, but their houses were ill contrived in other respects. It is astonishing
how they wasted room when they had little
to spare, and how completely they neglected
the important rule that every chamber should
be accessible without passing through another.
I do not believe that there is a mediæval house
in existence at all comparable to the best
modern ones for ingenuity of internal arrangement. Even the stone corkscrew staircases,
so common as to be almost universal in mediæval houses, are a most inconvenient kind of
staircase in use. As every step narrows till it
comes to nothing at the pillar, it is of use
only near the wall, and two people cannot
conveniently meet upon it. For carrying
large objects, such as pieces of furniture, a
corkscrew stair is the worst of all. From the

absence of proper landings there is an awk-
wardness at every door on the successive
stories. The only real advantages of these
stairs are that they occupy a minimum of
space on the ground plan, and that they produce a picturesque external effect when they
are built out in little towers with pepper-box
roofs. Sometimes the stair-turret is half lost
in the main building, sometimes it is entirely
absorbed and only the top of it visible. Something, however, is generally made of it in any
case. In the house in the Rue Cocand, mentioned above, the stair-turret is behind, and
only the top of it is seen; but it shows
well in the back yard, where it gives a good
finish to a picturesque accumulation of buildings on a small scale. In this house, as in
others of the same class, there is a predomi-
nant architectural feeling (as distinguished
from the business spirit of a mere builder),
which manifests itself in matters of detail.
There is hardly a bit of stone or wood in the
house, dating from its origin, that is not
treated with some intention of care and
taste.

In the region about the Cathedral there are
many good specimens of the old town-house

which would deserve to be illustrated. One
of them, belonging to the presiding judge, is
like two distinct buildings. It has a genuine
mediæval front to a court near one street,
and an interesting Renaissance front towards
another. The house occupied by M. Froment,
the well known artist, is entirely mediæval.
Some of the houses built against the town
wall have turned the old military towers to
account by making rooms in them. I know
a lady who has a pretty little boudoir in one of
these round towers, and amongst the arrangements of feminine taste and comfort it is easy
to forget the original intention of the building
till one is reminded of it by the thickness of
the wall as revealed by the depth of the window embrasure. The reader must not suppose
that the Gothic houses about the Cathedral
are rich in any striking architectural adornment. They are generally plain and substantial dwellings, with a few mouldings about
window and doorway, and perhaps an isolated
bit of sculpture here and there. With a single
exception, they are not on a large scale.

The exception is the Hôtel de Beauchamp,
which was purchased a few years ago by an
important archæological society — the Société

Éduenne — and classed as an historical monument, which insures its future preservation. It is a part, and only a comparatively small and unimportant part, of what was at one time an extensive Gothic palace. It belonged to Nicholas Rolin, Chancellor of Burgundy, who died in it in the year 1461. The main characteristics of it are a very highly pitched roof, lofty rooms, and one or two good chimney-pieces. It was occupied by work-people before the Société Éduenne bought it, and since the change of ownership it has been cleaned and carefully repaired, but not restored in any destructive sense. The greatest objection to what has been done is the substitution of a new roof of blue slate for the old common red tiles, which gave a pleasant warm contrast to the gray stone of the building. Blue slate is now extensively used in the old French provincial towns, which in the days before railways were happily preserved from it by their distance from slate quarries. It is at once the neatest, the coldest, and the hardest-looking of all materials for roofs. The bourgeois mind delights in its neatness, but it chills the heart of an artist.

The roof of the Hôtel de Beauchamp is so

steep and high that it contains rooms below the attics, being, in fact, itself divided into two stories, and the lower one is lighted by the dormer windows that are a conspicuous feature in the building. The Société Éduenne have taken the principal room for their meetings, and have arranged it with taste; the other large rooms are to be embellished gradually as the funds of the society permit, and filled with antiquities belonging to the society. Few associations of that kind have been so appropriately housed, and the luck in this instance is the more remarkable that what remained of the Hôtel de Beauchamp appeared to be doomed by the modern notion of alignement. It projects several feet into the street whose inhabitants eagerly looked forward to the day when the old building would be removed by the local ediles. That possibility ceased with its elevation to the rank of an historical monument. It is now tabooed, like the Roman gates and the Temple of Janus.

The bishop's palace includes some of the oldest mediæval buildings in the city, especially the tower of St. Léger (said to be eight hundred years old), but the mass of the build-

ing has been altered at the Renaissance.
There are some noble rooms in it, very lofty
and well lighted, and there is a fine staircase,
but, like most residences of the kind, its principal merits are those of space and convenience.
The garden is picturesque in the extreme,
with great varieties of level, some very fine
old trees, and a noble view of the near wooded
hills to the south. The preservation of St.
Léger's tower gives the bishop's palace great
dignity. Notwithstanding their generally destructive tendency, I have noticed that the
French often hesitate before destroying a
tower. There is an old one in the northern
mediæval wall of Autun, near the Avenue de
la Gare, which seemed doomed to destruction
as the ground was bought for building shops.
However, the purchaser preserved it, and
joined it to his new shop, only raising it a
little to the level of the new building and
roofing it afresh, of course with the now
inevitable slate.

I have said in another place that two parts
of the mediæval city were especially fortified,
— the citadel, in which stands the Cathedral,
and Marchaux, in the northeast corner, which
is the opposite corner diagonally. The march

of modern progress seems rather to have respected these old fortifications, for it so happens that the old houses which still remain are to be found chiefly in the citadel and in Marchaux. There is one at the foot of the clock-tower in Marchaux, the woodwork (of the sixteenth century) is well finished, and there is some carving in the interior; but tourists are respectfully informed that it would be useless for them to ask to see it, as the tenant has had it plastered up to escape the annoyance of untimely callers, being weary of the visits of the curious. The clock-tower has a bartizan reaching far down the east side of it, supported on the usual diminishing concentric mouldings, but under them in this instance there is the carved figure of a man. He is there still, but hidden, like the woodcarvings in the neighboring house, as a wall has been built against the tower just high enough to bury him. In the courtyard is a Gothic well, which in old times was adorned with a stone serving the office of a crane and projecting from the house wall. This is long since broken, but the remnant shows that it was richly and skilfully carved. The tower and well belonged, in fact, to one of the great

houses. As the citadel had its Hôtel de Beauchamp, so Marchaux had its Hôtel de Cluny.

In the street near it, the Petite Rue Marchaux, are several old houses in fair preservation. Close by, in the Grande Rue Marchaux,
are other old houses worth attention, and after
that the curious explorer finds a few others in
odd places here and there, but not in clusters
as about the Cathedral.

I only remember a single remaining example
of a bartizan in an ordinary house. It is at
the upper end of the Grande Rue Chauchien,
and is small, plain, heavy, and low. Bartizans
add greatly to the effect of towers, and give a
pretty architectural finish to corners even in
streets, but they should be of some height and
elegance. In the case mentioned, the bartizan
is overwhelmed by a high roof which rises far
above it, and is itself so near to the ground
that it seems almost as if it might incon-
venience the foot passengers.

There would be much more to say about
houses at Autun if we studied the changes in
domestic architecture down to modern days.
There are especially one or two curious examples of Renaissance work in which the
desire to have a complete composition of a

central *corps de bâtiment* with wings, and all
in a very small space, has led the architect to
erect wings so very narrow that it must be
impossible to use them for anything but
closets. Much building has been done during recent years, but it has rarely any pretension to architectural elegance; and it seems
not at all improbable that in the course of
the twentieth or the twenty-first century Autun
may once more cover the whole extent of
Augustodunum, and with streets rivalling the
straightness of the Roman ways. All that can
be said of the recently built houses is that
they excel their predecessors in light, healthi-
ness, and convenience. These are valuable
qualities, but when the last remnant of past
times has disappeared forever the artists and
archæologists of the future will hear the name
of Autun with regret; and if they visit the
site once covered by a great Gallo-Roman
city, and afterwards by a most picturesque,
though smaller, mediæval one, they will hardly
say, as Henri Martin, the historian, said lately,
that with the single exception of Paris, Autun
is even yet, by its site and character, " la plus
belle ville de France."